As the dust settled, Dawson got his first good look at the rustler.

He blinked. The rustler had lost his hat, exposing a head of curly blond hair. A pair of big Montana sky-blue eyes glared up at him from a face that left no doubt.

A woman rustler?

"You have to let me go," she snapped as the roar of the stampeding cattle died off in the distance.

"So you can finish stealing my cattle? I don't think so."

"You don't understand."

"The hell I don't. Where are they taking the cattle?"

She tested her left shoulder and grimaced.

"I think you'll survive," he said sarcastically.

She shot him a dirty look. "You could have killed me."

"It crossed my mind."

"Even after I saved you?" She narrowed those eyes at him like a gun.

"I beg your pardon?" He couldn't believe this woman.

"Do you think those cattle just happened to turn on their own?" She raised her chin as she said it, her gaze full of challenge. "I saved your life. Now you owe me."

USA TODAY Bestselling Author

B.J. DANIELS

RUSTLED

7038

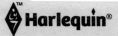

TORONTO NEW YORK LONDON
AMSTERDAM PARIS SYDNEY HAMBURG
STOCKHOLM ATHENS TOKYO MILAN MADRID
PRAGUE WARSAW BUDAPEST AUCKLAND

This book is for a good friend and fellow writer who is a huge fan of cowboys. My hat's off to Joanna Wayne, the woman who keeps those cowboys down in Texas finding the loves of their lives.

ISBN-13: 978-0-373-69555-3

RUSTLED

Recycling programs for this product may not exist in your area.

Copyright © 2011 by Barbara Heinlein

ABOUT THE AUTHOR

USA TODAY bestselling author B.J. Daniels wrote her first book after a career as an award-winning newspaper journalist and author of thirty-seven published short stories. That first book, *Odd Man Out*, received a four-and-a-half-star review from *RT Book Reviews* and went on to be nominated for Best Intrigue for that year. Since then she has won numerous awards, including a career achievement award for romantic suspense and many nominations and awards for best book.

Daniels lives in Montana with her husband, Parker, and two springer spaniels, Spot and Jem. To contact her, write to B.J. Daniels, P.O. Box 1173, Malta, MT 59538 or email her at bjdaniels@mtintouch.net. Check out her website at www.bjdaniels.com.

Books by B.J. Daniels

CAST OF CHARACTERS

Dawson Chisholm—The cowboy got more than he planned on when he caught one of the rustlers stealing his cattle.

Brittany Bo "Jinx" Clarke—If you let this cowgirl get her spurs into you, you're in for a wild ride.

Rafe Tillman—He liked to think he was the head of the rustling ring, but was there someone else giving the orders?

Hoyt Chisholm—Was it just bad luck with wives? Or was he guilty of murder?

Emma McDougal Chisholm—The fourth wife believed in her husband. Or was she just setting herself up to be his next victim?

Aggie Wells—The former insurance investigator was still missing and presumed dead—at least by most people.

Hank Thompson—He'd left the Double TT Ranch to his only son. But it came with strings attached.

Lyndel Thompson—He was running the Double TT into the ground.

Buck Clarke—Had the ranch manager known too much? Or was he just in the wrong place at the wrong time?

McCall Crawford—The sheriff had her hands full as it was with rustlers and missing women and baby making.

Chapter One

Dawson Chisholm reined in his horse to look back at the ranch buildings in the distance. This was his favorite view of the Chisholm Cattle Company. He'd always felt a sense of pride and respect for the ranching empire his father had built.

Today, though, he felt the weight of responsibility on his shoulders for the ranch and feared for his father—and the future. Someone wanted to destroy not only what Hoyt Chisholm had built, but Hoyt himself.

"I'm going to ride up into the high country and check the cattle on summer range," he'd told his five brothers. They knew him well enough to realize that as the oldest brother he needed some time alone after everything that had happened.

They'd been at the main house sitting around the kitchen table this morning, avoiding the dining room since their father had been arrested for murder and their stepmother, Emma, had taken off to parts unknown.

The house had felt too empty, so they had all moved back in even though they had their own houses on the huge ranch. When their father's new bride, Emma, had come to the house two months ago, she'd required them all to show up freshly showered and changed for supper every evening.

No one questioned Emma's new rules, which included no swearing in the house and bowing their heads in prayer before supper. In the weeks since she and Hoyt had wed, she'd made a lot of changes at Chisholm Cattle Company.

That was until the body of Hoyt's third wife turned up and he'd been arrested.

Dawson still couldn't believe it. There was no way his father was a murderer. Unfortunately, given the evidence against him and his wealth, the judge had denied bail and Hoyt was now sitting in jail in Whitehorse awaiting trial.

Emma... Well, she'd packed up and skipped town with only a short note saying she couldn't do this. It had broken their father's heart. Hoyt Chisholm had looked older than his fifty-six years when Dawson had visited him yesterday evening. He'd taken the news about Emma even worse than Dawson had thought he would.

"Emma wouldn't just leave," his father had argued. Emma had been nothing like his father's other wives. Redheaded with a fiery temper, plump and annoyingly cheerful. Her stepsons hadn't wanted to like her. But she'd won them all over and their father clearly adored her.

"She left a note, said she couldn't do this and packed up all her stuff and was gone when we got home," Dawson said, unable to hide his own anger—and not just at Emma. His father had gone off to a cattleman's meeting in Denver two months ago and, after a quick stop in Vegas, had come back with a wife. Why was his father surprised the woman would leave, under the circumstances?

"Listen to me," Hoyt said, leaning forward behind the thick piece of bulletproof glass as he spoke into the phone provided for inmates to talk to visitors. "Emma wouldn't leave. You have to find her."

Dawson didn't need this. He and his brothers were having a hard enough time running the ranch without their father. He had a lot more important things to do than find his father's fourth wife.

But, he had to admit grudgingly, he'd liked Emma and maybe that was why he was so angry with her for bailing on their father.

"Where would you suggest I look? Is there family I can call? Friends? Is she even from Denver?" When his father didn't answer any of the questions, he said, "You really don't know anything about her, do you?"

"I know she wouldn't leave me," Hoyt had snapped.

Dawson sighed now, took one last look at the ranch and spurred his horse into the thick cool darkness of the pines. The ride up from the main house had taken most of the day. The big blue sky overhead was tinted pink to the west where the sun had dipped behind the Bear Paw Mountains.

He breathed in the sweet scent of pine. Since he was a boy, he'd always come to the high country when life got to be too much down on the prairie. Having five brothers, all of them adopted by Hoyt years ago, not even a ranch as large as this one felt big enough sometimes.

"I need one of you to see if you can find Emma," he'd told his brothers before he'd ridden out.

"Dad just doesn't want to believe that she deserted him," Marshall had said. "What's the point in finding her? She won't come back."

"I'll go," Zane had said, speaking up. When they all looked at him as if he was crazy, he said, "Dad loves her. He has enough problems without worrying about Emma. I'll see if I can find her. Did he give you any place to start?"

"All we know is that he met her in Denver," Dawson had said. "I suppose you could start there."

None of them had any hope that Zane would find her. Even less hope that if he did, she would come back and stand by their father's side during his trial.

Dawson couldn't really blame Emma when he thought about it. Rumors had circled around Chisholm Cattle Company for years after Hoyt's first wife, Laura, had drowned on a Fork Peck Reservoir boating trip.

The rumors only got worse after his second wife, Tasha, had been killed on a runaway horse. When his third wife, Krystal, had disappeared, never to be seen again, people who knew him were convinced Hoyt Chisholm had the worst luck with wives. Others weren't so sure.

There was at least one person—an insurance investigator—who suspected that Hoyt Chisholm had not only murdered all three wives, but would also do the same with his latest, Emma.

Dawson knew better. Hoyt was his father, the man who had adopted three motherless boys—Colton, Logan and Zane when the triplets' mother had died in childbirth, father unknown. He'd adopted Dawson, Tanner and Marshall when their mother had abandoned them, father also unknown.

Hoyt probably would have adopted even more children who needed homes if it hadn't been for the trouble with his wives.

Dawson, the oldest, was three when his father married his second wife, Tasha. They had been married only a short time before her death. He was five when Krystal came into their lives. She'd stayed an even shorter time. He doubted his brothers, who were all a few years younger, remembered any of them.

After that their father had raised them alone. All six

of them now ranged from twenty-six to thirty-three. And then Hoyt Chisholm had met Emma.

A new wife had spurred all that old talk about Hoyt's other wives and brought former insurance investigator Aggie Wells back into their lives—until she'd gone missing. That was when their father's third wife's body had turned up. Aggie was still missing.

Dawson felt the temperature begin to drop up here in the mountains. He loved this ride from the sagebrush and prairie to the rocky mountain range, the towering pines and rush of snow-fed creeks. He'd been raised on a horse and felt as at home there as he did in the high country.

At heart he was a cattleman, he thought as he heard the comforting sound of cows lowing just over the ridge. There was nothing like that sound or seeing the herd scattered across a wide meadow.

He stopped a short way into the meadow and leaned on his saddle horn to admire the black cattle against the summer-green meadow. Chisholm Cattle Company raised the finest Black Angus beef there was—and lots of them.

At that moment he realized what a loner he was. Before Emma had left, he'd noticed that she'd seemed intent on seeing each of her stepsons settle down with the perfect woman. He shook his head at the thought. Was there a woman alive who could understand his need to ride up here and camp out for a few days with only cows as company?

He laughed at the thought, remembering some of the women he'd dated. Even hard-core country girls weren't all that up for roughin' it. He thought of the one woman he'd known who might have and quickly pushed the painful thought away.

A cold breeze stirred the deep shadows that had settled into the pine boughs. He glanced across the meadow to the spot where he usually camped and saw something move in the trees.

A hawk burst from a high branch. The cattle began to moo loudly and move restlessly in the bowl-like meadow. Something was spooking them. A mountain lion? A grizzly?

Dawson stared into the trees across the meadow and started to pull his rifle from the scabbard on his saddle, thinking it had to be a large predator for the cattle to get this nervous.

The first rider came out of the trees at a gallop. Dawson pulled his rifle as the rustler came into view and fired a shot into the air as warning before taking aim to fire another. The cattle began to scatter.

A second rustler appeared, then another and another broke from the pines; shots rang out across the grazing land as the rustlers tried to circle the now stampeding cattle.

Dawson realized the cattle were headed right for him—and so was one of the riders.

Chapter Two

With the stampeding cattle headed directly at him, Dawson realized there was nowhere to go to get away from them, and it was too late to try to outrun the herd. He was about to be caught in the middle of the stampede.

He reined his horse around in time to see one of the rustlers turn the herd at the last moment—and just enough that he was able to get out of the way. The cattle thundered past in a cloud of dust—the rustler with them.

Dawson sheathed his rifle, spurred his horse and took off after him. The rider was moving fast, bent over the horse and riding as if his life depended on it. It did, because Dawson was gaining on him. Just a few more yards…

Riding up behind him, Dawson dived off his horse, tackling the rustler. Both of them hit the ground at the edge of the thundering herd of cattle and rolled into the tall grass. Dust boiled up around them as they came to a stop at the base of a large pine tree, Dawson coming out on top.

As the dust settled, he got his first good look at the rustler. He blinked. A pair of big Montana-sky-blue eyes glared up at him from a face framed in blond curls.

A woman rustler?

"You have to let me go," she hollered as the roar of the stampeding cattle died off in the distance.

"So you can finish stealing my cattle? I don't think so."

"You don't understand."

"The hell I don't." He looked over his shoulder to see the last of the rustlers and cattle disappear through a gap in the trees. The rustlers had scattered the herd, but would still be able to cut out at least a hundred head.

He jerked the woman to her feet. "Where are they taking the cattle?"

She tested her left shoulder and grimaced, then she reached down to pick up her battered Western straw hat from the dirt.

"I think you'll survive," he said sarcastically.

She shot him a dirty look. "You could have killed me."

"It crossed my mind."

"Even after I saved you?" She narrowed those eyes at him.

"I beg your pardon?" He couldn't believe this woman.

"Do you think those cattle just happened to turn on their own?" She raised her chin as she said it, her gaze full of challenge. "I saved your life. Now you owe me. Let me go."

He laughed as he knocked the dust from his Stetson and settled it back on his head. "The only place you're going is to jail."

"That would be a mistake," she said meeting his gaze. Her eyes were a heartbreaking blue in a face that could stop traffic with its surprising beauty. She looked too sweet and innocent to be a rustler.

"What the hell are you doing rustling my cattle?" he demanded, although he'd bet it had something to do with a man. It usually did.

"You wouldn't believe me if I told you," she said, and glanced toward where the cattle had disappeared through a wide spot in the trees.

"Try me."

Something came into her eyes, a subtle look that warned him. He mentally kicked himself for not thinking of it sooner. She reached for the gun strapped to her hip, hidden under her long barn jacket.

He grabbed the weapon before she could, his eyes narrowing as he assessed her. So much for sweet and innocent.

She wasn't just a woman whose boyfriend had

talked her into some crazy stunt of rustling up a hundred head of cattle. The woman was armed and he'd already seen the way she could ride.

"How many others are there?" he demanded, grabbing a fistful of her jacket. "I think you'd better start talking before I tear into you."

She smiled. "I'm not sure you want to do that."

"Why is that?"

"You might not like the outcome."

He laughed again. He had a good ten inches on her and seventy pounds. She wasn't serious, was she?

Apparently she was, because before he could react, she punched him.

The blow caught him by surprise, breaking his hold on her and allowing her to take off running toward her horse, which had stopped a few dozen yards away.

Dawson went after her, bringing her down in the tall grass. She tried to fight him off, but he was onto her tricks this time and pinned her to the ground. He was suddenly aware of the soft curves.

"You have to listen to me." She ground out the words from between her gritted teeth. "You have to let me go. If you don't, they will come back for me and they will kill you. There are too many of them for you to fight off alone. You won't stand a chance and I don't want your blood on my hands."

"I'm touched by your concern for me. Especially after you just tried to pull a gun on me."

"I wasn't going to shoot you."

"You don't mind if I don't take your word on that, since you just punched me."

"You gave me no choice."

"Well, I'm giving you a choice now. Tell me how many of them there are."

She struggled under him for a few moments, then gave up and sighed. "Seven. How are those for odds?"

Not good. He'd heard about a large rustling ring that had been operating down in Wyoming and had only recently moved into southeastern Montana. He assumed it must be the same band of rustlers. Apparently they had now moved into north central Montana.

"When they realize I'm not with them, they will be back for me," she said.

Once the rustlers had the cattle settled wherever they planned to keep them for the night, they would come looking for this woman, sure as hell—if they didn't notice her missing sooner.

He wondered how badly they would want to find her and how long they would look when they didn't. He figured only one or two of them would return. The others would stay with the cattle. That at least would even the odds.

Also it would be dark soon. It got dark fast up here in the mountains. He had to make sure the band of rustlers didn't find them until he decided what to do.

Eventually he'd have to deal with the possibly that all of them might come back for her, depending on her relationship to this gang. Holding off seven of them wouldn't be easy. Especially with this woman to worry about. What *was* he going to do with her?

"Look, we don't have much time before they realize I'm not with them."

She had a point. He hauled her to her feet and walked her the rest of the way to his horse. Reaching into his saddlebag, he pulled out a length of rope.

"You can't tie me up."

"What would you suggest I do with you?"

"You work for Chisholm, right?" She took his silence for yes. "You really want to die for a hundred head of his cattle?"

He pulled her hands behind her back and began to tie her wrists together.

"You're making a huge mistake," she said.

"It won't be my first."

She was watching the edge of the trees where the last of the cattle and rustlers had disappeared. He could feel the tension running through her. She knew they would be coming back for her. He thought about his first impression—that some man had talked her into this.

"So who is he?" Dawson asked as he finished binding her wrists and turned her around to face him. "This cowboy who talked you into becoming a rustler?"

Her expression changed and her gaze shifted away, making him pretty sure he'd pegged this one right. But, hell, given what he'd seen of her, she could be the leader of this group. Still, he thought it was more likely that some man was involved.

"What did he promise you?" he asked when she said nothing. "Adventure? Money? A chance to go to prison?"

"Rustlers seldom go to prison, because they are seldom caught," she snapped, sounding angry.

"Well, I caught *you*," he said, just as angry, since she was right. Convictions of cattle thieves were rare to nonexistent and with cattle going for a thousand dollars a head and times being tough, the rustlers had gotten smarter. With open range where there were no fences to worry about and back roads poorly patrolled, all a thief needed was a horse, maybe a good cattle dog and a semitrailer. There was always a crooked cattle buyer for a quick sale, and they could walk away with some good money after very little work on their part.

These rustlers, though, were going for the big reward, rustling a hundred head at least. From what Dawson had seen so far, they knew exactly what they were doing. Just like this woman.

She cocked her head at him. "You caught me, but how are you going to keep me when the others come back?"

"Don't worry, I'll think of something." He dragged

her over to her horse. "Let me help you up," he said and, before she could protest, hoisted her up into her saddle. Taking her reins, he headed for his horse. "You try anything and you'll be on the ground again in a heartbeat. I don't think you want that, do you?"

She glared at him before looking again toward the opening in the trees as if she expected the other rustlers to come riding in at any moment.

Dawson knew what would happen if the rustlers caught them out in the open. He had to get her to the other side of the large meadow, to a place he'd found when he was a boy, a place where he could hide her and make sure she didn't warn her partners in crime.

He swung up onto his horse and, leading hers, headed across the meadow. He needed to get them both out of sight until he could decide what to do with her—and how to get his cattle back.

"If you let me go, I can keep them from coming back," she said. "You have my word."

"Your word, huh? Like that is worth anything."

She let out an unladylike curse as he led her and her horse across the meadow. "I'm just trying to save your sorry neck."

He glanced back at her. "And I'm just going after my cattle."

"*Your* cattle? Don't you mean your *boss's* cattle?"

"I'm one of those Chisholms who you think can afford to lose a hundred and twenty-five head of cattle without even noticing it."

"You're a *Chisholm?*"

He could tell she liked it better when she thought he was just one of the hired hands. "Dawson Chisholm, and you are…?"

"Everyone calls me Jinx."

He chuckled. "I can see why."

EMMA CHISHOLM WOKE WITH a terrible headache. She lay perfectly still and didn't dare open her eyes. There was a pounding at her temples and she felt sick to her stomach.

She inched her hand across the bed, hoping Hoyt was still lying next to her and hadn't gotten up early and gone to work already. Maybe if he got her something for her headache before she tried to get up—

The bed was empty. With a jolt she opened her eyes. Two thoughts hit her at once. She wasn't in her bed at the main house of Chisholm Cattle Company ranch and it wasn't morning.

Through the boards that had been nailed haphazardly over the only window in the room, she could see daylight, but from the angle of the shadows it appeared to be afternoon.

Emma struggled to sit up, taking in the unfamiliar small room with its paint-peeling faded walls, the mattress resting on the scarred wood floor, the tiny closet with two buckets, one full of water, and the tray near the door with a sandwich in plastic wrap, an apple and a thermos.

As her memory came back, she was suddenly aware of the cold air coming in through a broken pane at the window. She hugged herself for a moment before getting to her feet.

Her head swam and she had to drop back to her hands and knees. Crawling over to the tray, she opened the thermos. Coffee, and it was still hot. She poured herself some into the plastic cup it came with. Her fingers trembled as she took a sip and considered the situation she found herself in. It wasn't the first time she'd been drugged and locked in a room alone.

But it was the first time her captor had been a woman. Emma took another sip of the hot coffee to chase away the chill. She'd thought she'd been ready for Aggie Wells. She'd known the woman would come for her, but she'd underestimated Aggie.

When the former insurance investigator had disappeared a few weeks ago, Emma had been so certain Aggie was trying to make it appear that Hoyt had done something to her. But when Emma had recently come home from town and smelled the woman's perfume in the main house at the ranch, she'd known Aggie was alive.

She had wondered how Aggie had known that everyone was out of the house. That's when she'd found the listening devices Aggie had apparently installed in the house and she'd known that with Hoyt in jail and his six boys busy working on the ranch, it was only a matter of time before Aggie would come for her.

Emma remembered sitting in the kitchen after Hoyt was arrested, waiting to see what Aggie had planned next. She'd been sure that the woman's plan had been to frame Hoyt for the murder of his third wife—and then take advantage of Emma being alone at the ranch to what? Kill her?

Emma hadn't known, but she'd been armed and thought she was ready when Aggie suddenly appeared in the kitchen doorway.

Everything after that was still fuzzy. She drank more of the coffee, feeling a little better, unwrapped the sandwich—a ham and cheese—and took a bite before moving back over to the window and peering out a small hole the size of a fist between the boards.

Where was she? In some abandoned farmhouse near Whitehorse, Emma was fairly sure. The landscape looked familiar and she didn't think Aggie had driven far after she'd drugged her.

So what did Aggie have planned for her?

She thought about the first time she'd met the former insurance investigator at the bar at Sleeping Buffalo Resort north of town. She'd been surprised that Aggie was about her own age, early fifties, a tall, slim woman with an aura of intelligence and energy. Emma remembered thinking she was the kind of woman she could have been friends with—under other circumstances.

Aggie had told her that night about her suspicions that Hoyt Chisholm had killed his other three wives. Emma hadn't believed it. Still didn't, even though evidence had been found along with his third wife's remains that linked him to her murder.

She'd been all the more convinced of her husband's innocence when she'd realized that Aggie had faked her own disappearance to make Hoyt look guilty of yet another murder.

At a sound on the other side of the only door, Emma turned and braced herself. She didn't think Aggie planned to kill her—at least not yet. Otherwise, why bother to bring her here?

A dead bolt scraped in the lock, the knob turned and, as the door swung inward, Emma saw Aggie Wells framed in the doorway. She was holding a handgun in a way that made it clear she knew how to use it.

She laughed, because even if the woman had been unarmed, Emma wasn't up to launching any kind of attack.

"You're in a good mood," Aggie said. "But then you are annoyingly cheerful most of the time, aren't you? It is one of the things I hate about you."

"You mean there are other things you hate about me?" Emma said, pretending to be crushed.

"I hate that you're married to Hoyt Chisholm."

Now they were getting somewhere, Emma thought as she watched the woman come into the room. For some time, she had suspected that the reason Aggie was so obsessed about Hoyt's case was that she'd fallen in love with the man. Emma could understand how that might have happened. Look how quickly Emma herself had fallen for him.

"You should eat," Aggie said, sliding the tray toward her.

Emma sat down, reached for the thermos and started to pour herself another cup of coffee but stopped, the cup and thermos held in midair.

Aggie chuckled. "Don't worry, it's not drugged."

She finished pouring the rest of the coffee into the plastic cup, thinking it was too late anyway if the coffee was drugged. She returned the stopper to the thermos and sat back against the wall as she took a drink. The coffee made her feel a little better and she needed to start thinking straight.

The only way she could get herself out of this was if she was very careful with this crazy woman, who she suspected was also a killer.

Aggie had caught her off guard at the main house at the ranch this morning. It had been just this morning, hadn't it? She thought so. She'd been expecting her. She'd even gotten a small pistol out of Hoyt's gun safe.

But then Aggie had appeared in the kitchen doorway and said, "I think it's time I told you the truth."

Emma had held the gun on her as Aggie had sat

down across the table from her. "You framed my husband."

"I did much worse than that." Aggie had looked at Emma's coffee cup sitting on the table next to a small plate with cake crumbs on it. "I'll tell you everything, Emma. You deserve to know the truth. Is there any coffee?"

Emma thought she'd been watching Aggie the entire time she went to get another cup and the rest of the coffee in the pot. But that must have been when Aggie put the drug into her half-empty coffee cup.

Aggie had begun talking. Emma had listened, getting more drowsy by the moment and having a hard time making sense of what the woman was saying. It wasn't until she'd dropped her coffee cup that she realized she'd been drugged. She'd grabbed for the gun, but her movements had been too slow by then and Aggie had been much quicker.

She remembered Aggie walking her out to an old pickup and buckling her in. Emma couldn't be sure how far they had gone when Aggie got her out and up the stairs into the old farmhouse. That's the last she remembered until waking up thinking it was morning.

"What now?" Emma asked as she picked up the sandwich and took a bite.

"We wait," Aggie said.

"What for?"

Aggie merely smiled and turned to leave.

"You realize my family will be looking for me," Emma said.

"I wouldn't count on that. You left a note that said you couldn't deal with all of this."

"Hoyt won't believe it," she said with more confidence than she felt.

"Oh, I think he will. Along with the note, everything you brought into the marriage is gone from the house. If they bothered to check, which I don't think they will, they'd find that you bought a used pickup the day after Hoyt was arrested. The title is in the name of Emma Chisholm."

ZANE HAD NO IDEA HOW to find Emma. He started his search in Denver because that was where his father had met her. He flew into the mile-high city on the last flight out of Billings.

The cattleman's meeting had been held at one of the large hotels downtown. He had booked a room, feeling as if he was searching for a needle in a haystack. Armed with a photo of Emma taken at the ranch, he began with employees at the hotel.

"You a cop or a bill collector?" one of the clerks behind the main desk asked him.

"She's my stepmother," he said truthfully. "She's gone missing."

"And you think she's hiding out here at the hotel?"

"No, but I think she stayed here the beginning of May." Zane leaned closer and dropped his voice. "I didn't want to get into this, but...she met my father here, they eloped days later to Vegas and now she's disappeared and I haven't a clue how to find her."

"What about your father? He doesn't know how to find her either?"

"Seems they saw no reason to share their pasts or much else."

The clerk didn't look as if he believed a word of it.

"I just need to make sure she's all right," he said. "My father is worried about her." He laid a fifty-dollar bill on the counter, his hand covering all but the important parts of it. "Any help you can give me would be greatly appreciated."

"I didn't work here then, but I could take a look and see if she was registered back in May," the clerk said, smoothly cupping the fifty in his palm as Zane removed his hand. He tapped on the computer keyboard.

"It would have been under Emma McDougal."

The clerk skimmed the computer screen. "Nope. Sorry. No Emma McDougal registered as a guest here in the month of May. Or April, for that matter."

Now all Zane had to go on was what little had been on the marriage license he'd found in his father's safe. Apparently Emma had been born in Caliente Junction, California, fifty-three years ago. He'd looked on the internet. Caliente Junction was now nothing more than a wide spot in the road. Even if someone still lived there, which looked doubtful from what he'd seen, what were the chances anyone there would even remember her or her family?

Zane went to his room and called home to tell his brothers where he was headed in the morning.

"Where the hell is Caliente Junction?" Marshall asked.

"Apparently out in the desert near the Salton Sea. I don't think there is a town there—if there ever was—from what I can tell. Just a few buildings on a two-lane road. What's going on there?"

"Just working. Dawson is still up in the mountains," his brother said. "You know him, he heads for high ground the moment there's trouble at the ranch. Nothing new there. Let us know what you find out about Emma. Dad keeps harping on us to find her."

Zane hung up and booked a flight into Palm Springs, California, for the next morning as he considered Caliente Junction on his laptop screen. He had a bad feeling his father wasn't going to like what he found out about his new bride.

JINX CLARKE RODE ALONG just feet from Dawson Chisholm, frantically trying to decide what to do. Her options were limited given that her hands were tied behind her and he was holding her horse's reins. One false move and, as he said, she'd be hitting the dirt again. Her left shoulder hurt as it was from her recent fall, thanks to him. She wasn't looking forward to being thrown to the ground again.

But she knew that at any moment Rafe could come riding out of the trees with all but a couple of his men with him. If he noticed she wasn't with them, he would hightail it back for her. More than likely, though, he wouldn't know they'd lost her until they got the cattle down to the first corral.

Which meant it would be some time before anyone would realize she was missing. But Rafe would come back. Even if he came alone, Dawson Chisholm was a dead man.

Jinx studied him as he led her across the wide meadow, trying to decide how much to tell him. The cattleman had coal-black hair and the darkest eyes she'd ever seen. She guessed he had some Native American in him. He was also handsome as sin—not that she would admit to noticing.

What worried her was why he'd shown up when he had. Either his timing was just his bad luck or it was no coincidence. It had been her idea to hit the Chisholm Cattle Company, because she'd thought it was big enough that they wouldn't be coming across anyone. But now she wondered if Rafe hadn't gone along with it too easily.

"So what's your real name?" Dawson asked, glancing back at her again. "I like to know who I'm dealing with."

"Jinx is all you get, Chisholm," she said.

He shook his head as if she was the most contrary woman he'd ever known. Clearly he hadn't known many women, if that was the case. "The sheriff will get your name out of you."

Jinx groaned. If he thought he could scare her with threats of the sheriff, he was sadly mistaken. She was far more worried about the killers she'd been riding with—and the dark-haired cattleman who had her tied and bound.

"I didn't check to see if you had some sort of identification on you," he was saying. "We might be able to settle this a whole lot quicker than waiting for the sheriff."

"Do you really think I'm stupid enough to carry identification on me?" she snapped.

"Do you really think I'm stupid enough to believe anything you say? At this point, you don't have a lot of credibility with me."

Neither did he with her. "How is it you just happened to show up when we were about to rustle your cattle, Chisholm?"

"Just luck, I guess," he said without turning to look at her.

She saw that they had reached the other side of the meadow and he was now leading her horse through the trees and up the mountainside to an outcropping of rocks. Did he think he could hold off seven men from there?

"These men I'm riding with are dangerous. When they come back for me—"

"What makes you so sure they'll be back for you?" he asked. "I'm surprised they even let a woman ride with them to begin with. A woman would be a liability. Especially one named Jinx."

Her temper flared from the insult. "I can ride with the best of men."

He chuckled. "I noticed. But I would imagine it took more than that to get into a group of men like this one."

She knew what he was insinuating and wished she could kick him where it would hurt the most. It hadn't been easy getting in with the rustling ring. She'd had to lie, cheat and steal. Fortunately that was as far as she'd had to go once she caught Rafe's attention at a bar down in Big Timber.

Rafe wasn't the ringleader. He got his orders from someone else. But he was the one the others listened to. He'd put up a fight for her. The other rustlers riding with him hadn't wanted a woman along, so she'd had to prove herself in their eyes. It wasn't enough that she could ride a horse and shoot. She had to have something they needed—information. She'd given them Chisholm Cattle Company.

Jinx grimaced at the realization that she was the one who was responsible if Dawson Chisholm got killed—and the way things were going there was nothing she could do to stop it.

Unless there was a chance Dawson was working with Rafe. That would explain why he was here. She wouldn't let herself worry about that right now. She had to keep her eye on her goal. Nothing could stop her. Not Rafe and all his men or this good-looking cattleman. When she got what she'd wanted, it would have all been worth it.

But as she stared at the determined set of Chisholm's broad shoulders, she wondered how high the price was going to get before this was over.

Chapter Three

Emma finished the sandwich. Her mind had been racing since Aggie left her alone in the small room of the abandoned old farmhouse. She'd listened, wondering if the woman was also staying here in this house. Where else could she be staying with every law enforcement officer in the state looking for her?

Glancing toward the window, Emma considered using the tray the next time Aggie left it to try to pry off the boards. It would be no easy task, since someone—probably Aggie—had nailed them on with large nails that would be hard to remove even with a claw hammer.

Not to mention what Emma would do after that. It was a two-story house. Was she going to throw out the mattress, then throw herself after it?

Thinking of ways to escape was better than considering why Aggie had left her alive. What was she waiting for?

Emma's first guess would have been Hoyt making bail. Once he was out, if Emma ended up dead, that would pretty much seal his fate. Somehow Aggie would plant evidence, as she had with Hoyt's third wife's body, to make him look guilty of her death, as well.

But Hoyt hadn't been able to make bail. Did Aggie have something planned to get him out?

And what was her motive for *any* of this? If Aggie had fallen in love with Hoyt, as Emma speculated, then why send him to prison for murder? It didn't make any sense unless… With a start, she realized why. What if they weren't dealing with a sane woman? Stalking Hoyt to the point where she'd lost her job certainly made Aggie look more than a little crazy.

From what Emma had been able to find out, Aggie had become obsessed with the insurance investigation into the death of Laura Chisholm, Hoyt's first wife. It had been ruled an accidental drowning, but since the body was never found…

When Hoyt's second wife had died, that must have been enough to make Aggie reopen the first wife's case.

So was that the problem? She was dealing with an insane woman bent on proving Hoyt was a killer—no matter the cost?

Her head still ached from the drugs and she was glad Aggie hadn't seen fit to drug her again. Which meant there were no other houses nearby, no chance of anyone just happening by, no one to hear her calling for help. So she would save her breath. Not that she was a screamer anyway.

Emma had learned early in life to accept things the way they were, good or bad. Wasn't that why she hadn't wanted to know Hoyt's past—because she hadn't wanted to tell him about her own?

THE CAVE WAS ON THE SIDE of the mountain, but few if any people knew about it. Dawson had found it on one of his trips up to the summer range when he was a boy. He'd been following a buck deer that had disappeared near the entrance. He'd almost missed seeing the opening for the overgrown brush. He'd put some of the brush back after he'd explored the cave, wanting to keep it a secret even from his brothers.

As he led the horses up into a stand of pines below the hidden cave entrance, he kept his eyes and ears alert for any sign of the rustlers. The sun had dipped behind the trees, forming deep shadows beneath them. The air had turned colder, as it did up here in the mountains.

"This is a mistake," Jinx said as he hauled her off the horse.

"You're the one who made the mistake when you decided to rustle my cattle."

She sighed deeply. "If you let me go, I will lead them away from you. I can tell them my horse stepped into a hole and I got thrown." She cocked her head at him. "I look like I got thrown to the ground, don't I?"

He glanced at her dusty clothing. There was a smudge of dirt on her cheek, her hat was crooked from where she'd hastily put it back on her head and her short curly blond hair had a twig in it. He removed the twig and tossed it over his shoulder.

"They'll come for me tonight. You can't hold off seven of them."

"Maybe. Maybe not."

"Isn't your life worth more than cattle?" she demanded.

"This isn't about money. Or even cattle. It's about defending what is yours."

She raised an eyebrow and glanced at his left hand. "Who was she?"

"I beg your pardon?"

"The woman you lost to someone else."

Dawson turned his back to her as he ground tied the horses.

"It must have been serious. High school sweetheart? Fiancée? Wife?" She let out a low laugh. "You didn't fight for her and you've regretted it ever since. So now you're damned sure going to fight for your cattle because of it. Is that it?"

He turned to face her. "You make a better rustler than a psychotherapist. Come on," he said, picking up his saddlebags. "I'm hungry and want to get something to eat before your friends come back. *If* they come back for you. Either way, I'm going after my cattle in the morning at first light."

JINX STARED AT HIS BACKSIDE as he started up the hill. Damn this cocky rancher. He acted as if he'd completely forgotten about her, but she wasn't fooled. This long, tall cowboy was aware of her every move, she thought as she started after him. She had no choice right now.

He could deny it all he wanted, but she was sure he'd lost some woman, a woman who'd hurt him badly. Because of it, he'd be happy to tackle her to the ground again. In fact, he'd take some pleasure in it.

She knew better than to try to make a run for it with her hands tied behind her and it getting dark. She'd be lucky if she didn't run into a tree and kill herself.

No, she had to wait, bide her time. Chisholm would make a mistake and she would get away. She had to. She'd come too far to let anyone stop her now. There had to be a way to get around this cocky cowboy—after all, he was a man.

And, oh, what a man, she thought as she studied him. Broad shoulders, slim hips, long denim-clad legs. Not to mention his face. Chiseled strong features, those dark, bottomless eyes and the way his lips quirked up on one side when he looked at her.

She wondered about the woman who'd broken his

heart and made him the way he was. She must have been a beauty, probably some city girl who would have eventually left him anyway.

Jinx hated her stab of resentment at the thought of the kind of woman a man like Dawson Chisholm would have fallen for. She swore under her breath. How different she and that woman would have been.

She turned her thoughts to how to get away from him. She'd do whatever she had to because she couldn't let this man stop her. One way or another, she was going to get what she'd promised her father on the day she buried him.

Telling Chisholm the truth was out of the question. She couldn't chance it. It bothered her that he didn't seem worried about fighting off seven rustlers, and made her suspicious that he knew he wouldn't have to because he was in on this and was now waiting, like her, for Rafe to return.

The only thing that Jinx did believe about Chisholm was that he was angry about a woman riding with the rustlers. If he was in cahoots with Rafe, she had a feeling he planned to have it out with the rustler.

Either way, she was in trouble. Rafe liked to think of himself as the leader of the rustlers, but she knew better. And Chisholm must, too. If he demanded Rafe get rid of her, then Rafe would buckle like a bad saddle under the weight.

A sudden shiver of fear quaked through her as she

had another thought. What if somehow they'd found out who she really was? She'd seen how surprised Dawson Chisholm had been when he'd tackled her. He hadn't expected her to be riding with the others. Or had he?

If he already knew, then that would explain why Chisholm had shown up when he had. He'd come up here to make sure she was stopped.

Unless she could stop Chisholm first.

EMMA CURLED UP on the mattress on the floor and pulled the blankets Aggie had thoughtfully provided over her. She could hear Aggie moving around somewhere in the house. She still felt woozy from the drug she'd been given.

At the sound of footfalls on the stairs, Emma sat up, holding the blankets to her chin as if they would protect her, and waited. The door opened. Aggie stood silhouetted in the doorway.

"You awake?"

"Yes," Emma said. "Not that the accommodations aren't delightful."

Aggie stepped into the room, closed the door and stood against it. Emma could barely see her in the dim light that came through the hole between the boards over the window.

"I like you," Aggie said. "I'm not going to hurt you."

"That's good." She figured she knew what was coming next.

"But I can't let you go back to the house and Hoyt."

"Why is that?" Emma asked.

Aggie let out an exasperated sigh. "I've told you. It's too dangerous."

"We both know that Hoyt is not a killer."

To her surprise Aggie said, "You could be right."

Was the woman merely trying to pacify her?

"Aggie, if you turn yourself in—"

She let out a laugh. "I haven't done anything."

Emma would beg to differ. "You abducted me, drugged me and are holding me prisoner."

"For your own good."

Now it was her turn to laugh. "And who are you protecting me from, Aggie?" When she didn't answer, Emma said, "Hoyt didn't kill anyone."

She heard Aggie slide down to sit on the floor and thought about trying to overpower her. But she knew that by the time she threw off the blankets and got up and launched herself at the woman, Aggie would be ready for her. Aggie was armed, probably with the same gun she'd been carrying earlier, and Emma wasn't in the mood for a suicide mission.

Also a part of her hoped that Aggie was finally going to tell her the truth.

"Do you know why I was such a good insurance investigator?" Aggie asked, seemingly out of the blue. She didn't wait for Emma to answer. "I studied everything about the people involved, and not just the surviving spouse. I wanted to know the deceased as intimately as if that person was alive."

"You're saying you got to know Hoyt's other wives?" Emma said. She had wondered what they had really been like. Nothing like herself, she would bet. They were probably tall, willowy and beautiful, not to mention young.

"I'm not sure Hoyt knew Laura as well as I have come to know her," Aggie said. "I could say the same for his two other wives, as well. But Laura…" She sighed. "She was like you, apparently totally enamored by Hoyt. At first. But I'm sure you've heard about how close the emotions are between love and hate."

"If you're telling me she grew to hate him, I don't believe you. I can't imagine anything Hoyt could have done that would have—"

"She believed he'd fathered his first three sons."

"I don't believe it. A simple DNA test would prove—"

"There wasn't DNA testing yet when Laura died."

"But there is now. And anyway, if he was the biological father to those boys, Hoyt would have admitted it."

"Why do you keep defending him?"

"Because I love him." She waited for Aggie to admit her own feelings for Hoyt. She heard the woman get to her feet again and quickly said, "I think you fell for him, as well." She didn't add that she thought Aggie had killed his other wives because she was jealous.

"I'll admit your husband is…charming. But historically, he is also dangerous to be around."

Not half as dangerous as you are, Emma thought. "So you're just trying to protect me," she said as she heard Aggie open the door to leave.

Aggie chuckled but didn't respond.

Emma lay back down on the mattress and pulled the blankets over her, but she couldn't fight off the chill Aggie had left in the room.

DAWSON HEARD JINX behind him. She was as sure-footed as an expensive filly as she climbed up to the cave. He told himself that he could almost hear the wheels in her head turning. She would try to get away when the rustlers came back for her. Or at the very least, give away their location—if he let her. He was already outnumbered. He'd have to find a way to even the odds.

As he moved a piece of dried brush away from the entrance to the cave, he heard her come up beside him. He turned on his flashlight and shone it into the cavern. To his relief it wasn't occupied by any animals.

"Ladies first," he said with more gallantry than he felt.

She smirked at that as she bent to step through the small opening. Once inside, she stood to her full height of about five-seven.

Dawson stepped past her, going around a corner in the cave to the hidden cavern room. As he lit the kerosene lantern he'd left there on one of his trips to the high country, she followed him.

In the golden light he studied her, wondering what she'd try next. The one thing he knew for sure, there was plenty of fight left in this woman. He'd have to watch her closely or suffer the consequences.

"What now, Chisholm?" she asked as she glanced around. He could see that she'd been surprised by the size of the cave, surprised that he'd furnished it over the years with not only a lantern but with a cot, a collapsible table and stool, a few pots and pans and a Coleman stove.

"Sit down over here and take a load off," he said, opening the folding stool he used when he came up here.

"Take a load off, Chisholm?" she asked with amusement. She was slim, curved in all the right places, and she knew it.

"So to speak," he amended.

He didn't go far from the cave, not trusting her, but he had to take care of their horses. When he returned with some firewood, he found her sitting where he'd left her, which surprised him. But he didn't doubt she'd taken a look around for something to cut the rope binding her wrists behind her. Before he'd left he'd been smart enough to make sure there was nothing sharp she could use.

The way the cave was structured, the opening turned just inside, which meant that light from the stove or a fire couldn't be seen from the meadow. The cave was ventilated through a crack at the back that opened to fresh air on the cliff above them, so the smoke from a fire would draft upward high on the cliffs, on the same principle as a fireplace in a home.

If and when the rustlers returned for Jinx they might catch a whiff of smoke, but they would never be able to find the cave. He doubted they would even smell the smoke if they stayed down in the meadow.

He made a small fire at the back of the cave near the vent and close to Jinx. It would be getting cold once the sun went down. Then he started the Coleman stove and dug some food out of his saddlebag.

This cave had been a retreat for years, his own private sanctuary in the high country. A part of him resented that he'd had to bring her here, resented it even more when she asked, "So you come up here and play house by yourself a lot?"

He shot her a warning look before concentrating again on his cooking. He figured she was right about the other rustlers coming back to look for her—but not for a while, he thought. They'd have to secure the cattle. It would take a while for them to even realize they'd lost her after all that confusion earlier.

Dawson suspected that the main reason they would come back for her was that they wouldn't trust her. At least one of them, the boyfriend, would have another motive.

But given all that, he felt they were relatively safe in the cave, at least for the time being. He'd hidden the horses around the side of the mountain and covered the opening to the cave again with the dried brush. Even if they were found, the cave was high enough on the mountainside that he could hold them off for a long time. He hadn't brought an arsenal, but he always had extra ammunition.

"Dawson," she said, using his first name in a way that reminded him of melted honey and put him on guard. He'd been expecting her to make some kind of move and shouldn't have been surprised that she'd chosen this one.

"I don't want to see you get killed," she said, sweet enough to give him a toothache. "Maybe there is some way we can work this out so we both get what we want."

"I guess that depends on what you want," he said, not turning around. He heard her get up and come toward him and was glad he'd tied her hands behind her back. Otherwise he'd be worried about getting his head bashed in.

"All I need is for you to let me go."

"How would that get me back my cattle?" he asked, playing along.

"Well," she said softly right behind him. "If you just untie me…"

JINX LOWERED HERSELF to the cave floor next to him. He glanced over at her, eyes narrowing a little as she repeated his first name, her voice dripping with sugar. She saw the male spark in his eye as she moved closer. How sad that men were so much alike, she thought, a little disappointed in this one. She thought he was too smart to let himself be seduced by her.

She hated that she'd had to resort to such distasteful behavior, but too much was at stake. If she had to use her feminine wiles, she would.

"Yes?" He was close enough that she caught his very masculine scent.

She moved so her thigh brushed his. "Why don't we be honest with each other?"

"Why don't we?" He pressed his thigh against hers. His leg felt warm, even through his jeans. His dark eyes locked with hers. She felt a shiver that she quickly squelched. His eyes were golden like a big cat in the firelight. He really was magnificent.

It was the intellect in that gaze that gave her pause. She saw challenge in his eyes as well as a warning. This was a man you didn't want to fool with.

"Tell me what you're really doing up here," she

said, not about to break eye contact first. He might be dangerous, but then again, he didn't realize the kind of woman he'd crossed paths with either.

"Checking my cattle, just like I told you."

He was either telling the truth or he was a damned good liar.

She reminded herself that he could just be playing along. If he knew who she was and what she was doing on his land… "Can't you please untie me?"

"No."

"You really think I'm going to get away?"

He smiled. "If I give you half a chance, yes." He turned back to his cooking.

"There wasn't another reason you just happened to come up here?" she asked quickly.

He turned off the stove and gave her his full attention. She found herself holding her breath. There was something about this man that scared her—especially the way he made her heart pound when he was this near, his gaze so intent on her that she feared he could see into her soul.

"As a matter of fact, there was another reason."

She expected him to finally tell her that he knew who she was. That she was the reason he was here.

"I wanted to spend a few days up in this country because I enjoy it. I thought I'd be alone. But since I'm not…" He was taunting her. Her feminine wiles were wasted on this man. "So, Jinx, what exactly are you offering?"

"If you think I'm going to sleep with you, you're going to be disappointed," she snapped and slid away from him.

He laughed. "Hell, I'm already disappointed. I thought we were being honest with each other."

"I should just let them kill you," Jinx grumbled, trying to get to her feet. With her hands tied behind her, it was a struggle.

Dawson rose abruptly, grabbed her waist and lifted her to her feet. His dark gaze bored into hers. "Now that we're being honest, no more games. Seduction might have worked on your rustler boyfriend, but quite frankly you aren't very good at it and anyway, you're not my type."

She swore as she tried to kick him in the groin. He'd obviously expected it, because he stepped to the side, grabbing her as she lost her balance and started to fall to the cave floor.

"Enough foreplay," he growled as he hauled her back over to the stool and pushed her down on it. Leaning over her, his gaze fired with anger as he said, "I'm getting my cattle back and you're going to jail, and if your boyfriend comes after you, he's going to get himself killed."

Chapter Four

Zane was too anxious to just sit around in his hotel room. He'd booked a flight to Palm Springs for the morning, but there was nothing more he could do today.

As he rode down in the elevator to the lobby, he noticed a woman going into the bar. She was probably in her forties, alone and wearing something provocative.

He was instantly reminded that his father had met Emma here in this hotel. What had she been doing here if she hadn't been a guest? As he stepped into the darkness of the bar, it took a moment for his eyes to adjust before he saw the woman who had gotten him thinking.

She had taken a stool at the bar and was now leaning toward the young male bartender, giving him a glimpse of her cleavage and asking him what he would suggest.

"I can make you a nice mango margarita," he said.

She smiled. "That sounds nice."

Zane took a stool down the bar from the woman.

"I'll be right with you," the bartender called to him.

Looking around, he saw that the bar was fairly empty, but then again by bar time standards, it was early. There was a couple at a table toward the back, two businessmen at another table and a lone fifty-something man at the other end of the bar who had noticed the woman. She was hard to miss.

This was a scene Zane had seen played out many times before. Pretty soon the man would offer to buy the woman another mango margarita. She'd accept. He would move down the bar and strike up a conversation with her before taking the stool next to her.

Is this how his father had met Emma, Zane wondered with disgust. Had she been trolling the hotel bar?

He had a hard time believing that, given what little time he'd spent around Emma. But that was the problem. None of them actually *knew* Emma. That had become clear the moment he'd started looking for her. It could be that she was one of those women who kept reinventing themselves.

The bartender came down the bar, set a cocktail napkin in front of him and asked, "What can I get you?"

"A bottle of beer," Zane said. "Something local would be great."

"Dark or light?"

"Dark."

The bartender returned with a bottle of dark beer and set it down along with a frosted glass.

"Maybe you can help me," Zane said. He saw the bartender tense. "I'm looking for someone."

"Isn't everyone?"

"This woman," he explained as he pulled out the snapshot of Emma taken at the ranch.

The bartender glanced at the photo. Zane could tell he was ready to say he'd never seen the woman before, but something stopped him. He picked up the photo.

"What about her?" he asked.

"So she used to come in a lot?"

The bartender laughed and glanced down the bar, apparently catching Zane's drift. The lone drinker had skipped part of the script and had moved right in, pulling up a stool next to the woman.

"You're barking up the wrong tree," the bartender said. "Emma McDougal worked here at the hotel, at the front desk. As far as I know, she didn't drink." He tossed the photo back at Zane. "She's a nice woman. Everyone liked her. We were happy for her when we heard she'd fallen in love and gotten married. Is there any reason we shouldn't be happy for her?"

"I don't know. She's disappeared."

The bartender looked concerned. "And you're looking for her because...?"

"She's married to my father. He's worried about her, convinced she wouldn't just take off."

"No, she wouldn't. Unless she was forced to for some reason." The bartender glared at Zane. "Was there some reason?"

"My father adores her."

"Then you'd better find Emma, because I have a bad feeling she's in trouble," he said as the man down the bar ordered another mango margarita for his companion.

JINX HID HER EMBARRASSMENT under her anger at herself for pulling such a stunt. She should have known better than to try to seduce the arrogant bastard, but she was desperate. She had to get away from him. As she watched him calmly go back to his cooking, she was all the more convinced he was toying with her. But was it because he knew who she was and why she was here?

Or because he thought her just another rustler and he was just another rancher about to lose his cattle and his life?

Well, if that was the case, then there was nothing she could do about it. She had tried to warn him. Now the smug cattleman was on his own.

She swore under her breath as she saw him tilt his head as if listening. Rafe *would* come looking for her, she was sure of that. The man he worked for wouldn't like there being any loose ends. The rustlers had already killed at least one rancher who got in their way on the orders of whoever was leading this gang. Even if she'd been thrown from her horse and broken her neck, Rafe would have to make sure she was dead so he could report back to his boss.

Chisholm moved around the corner of the cave to look out the entrance. She knew he was looking toward the trees where the cattle and rustlers had disappeared. Getting up, she stepped around the corner of the cave so she could see out.

A dusky gray light had fallen over the meadow, giving it an eerie feel. It was deceptive. She thought she saw ghostlike riders coming out of the mist only to have them evaporate before her eyes.

A darkness had settled in the pines even though it would still be light for several hours. She was surprised Rafe hadn't come back. Was it possible he hadn't realized yet that she was missing? Or was he too busy making sure the cattle were taken care of first?

Her being missing would spook all of them. Maybe they would decide to drive the cattle farther than planned.

She shifted her focus to Dawson Chisholm. What was he planning to do with her? She hated to think.

As he started to turn back in her direction, she quickly moved to her stool and sat down again, her mind racing. She had to find a way to hook back up with the rustlers before they became more suspicious of her.

Dawson went back to minding the meal he was making. She felt her stomach growl. She hadn't eaten since breakfast and the bacon he was frying smelled wonderful. Her stomach growled loudly and she saw him smile to himself as if he'd heard.

"Apparently it's a good thing you decided to ride up here when you did," she said as she watched him cook. He was making some kind of dough and now dropped it into the sizzling fat. Fry bread. She groaned inwardly as the smell filled the cave.

"Apparently it was. I'd heard about a band of rustlers operating near the Montana border down by Wyoming, but I didn't realize they'd worked their way this far north."

So he *had* heard. Had he also heard about the man who'd been killed down in Wyoming, his house burned to the ground by the rustlers?

"So how exactly did you pick my ranch?" he asked pointedly.

"What makes you think *I* had anything to do with the decision?"

He smiled. "I guess it's just my suspicious nature."

"Kind of like mine. Out of all the ranches around Whitehorse, you somehow knew yours would be hit next by rustlers? Maybe you knew before I did."

He laughed. "If you're insinuating that I'm somehow connected to the rustlers you're riding with—"

"That's exactly what I'm thinking. Chisholm Cattle Company is family owned. Six brothers, right? All adopted." She narrowed her eyes at him. "Wouldn't be unusual for one of the brothers to feel he was owed more than he was getting."

He chuckled. "You'll play any card, won't you? This tactic isn't going to work any better than the others you've tried." He turned the bread from the small pan onto the two strips of bacon he'd fried and folded the bread into a sandwich. He started to take a bite, but stopped as he glanced at her.

"Hungry?" he asked, even though he knew darned well that she was.

"No," she snapped, but her stomach growled loudly again, giving her away.

He laughed, pushed himself up and walked over to look down at her. He wiped the dust from a corner of the table and set down the sandwich. Then he untied her wrists, freeing one hand and tying the other to her leg.

"You really are the least trusting man I've ever met," she said as he put the sandwich into her free hand.

"Let's not forget that you and I only met because you were rustling my cattle."

She cocked her head at him. "You wouldn't have trusted me even if we'd met at church, and you know it."

His gaze met hers and held it for a long moment. "You might be right about that."

As he walked back to the Coleman, out of the corner of his eye he watched Jinx take a bite of the sandwich. She moaned with pleasure and licked her fingers as some of the bacon grease tried to get away.

Dawson smiled, liking her more than he had, definitely more than he wanted to, as he started more fry bread for himself. The atmosphere in the cave seemed to have warmed considerably.

"Thank you," she said when she'd finished eating, licking her fingers before wiping her hand on her jeans.

"You're welcome." They sat around the cave in silence as he cooked and ate. He watched her, still afraid she would try to get away, but she seemed to have realized there was no way he was going to let that happen.

The crackling flames flickered, sending long shadows over the cave walls. The scent of the pine trees mixed with the smell of bacon and fried bread. The air had cooled outside the cave. Tonight would be cold. This high in the mountains was always cold at night even in the summer months.

He let the fire die down to hot embers as he considered the best way to get his cattle back. Making the long ride out to the ranch for help was out of the question. By then, the cattle and the rustlers would be gone.

He had no way to contact the ranch, since even if he carried a cell phone, it wouldn't have worked up here. Cells phones worked within only about ten miles of Whitehorse. After that, you were on your own.

Glancing over at Jinx, he knew she was his biggest problem. His every instinct told him not to trust her an inch. This was no small rustling operation, which meant there was a lot of money involved and whoever was behind it knew way too much about the ranchers—and cattle—they were going after. That worried him.

The rustlers he'd known hadn't been organized. They'd acted more on impulse, often after a few beers at the bar. But then, he'd never seen as large a gang as this one. Definitely not one with a woman riding along.

He remembered how much she'd known about the Chisholm ranch and his family. It galled him that anyone would hit Chisholm Cattle Company. He was more interested in getting his cattle back than trying to get justice, but just the fact that they'd hit his ranch made him dig his heels in. He wanted these bastards caught—including whoever was behind them.

He didn't doubt there was someone who was the brains of the band of rustlers who stayed behind the scenes, the man with the crooked cattle buyer contacts who financed the semitrucks and trailers needed for an operation this big.

But how was he going to get his cattle back, catch the rustlers and keep this woman from getting away?

He studied Jinx, wondering if she had realized yet that he planned to get his cattle back—even if it meant using her to do it.

IT WAS DARK BY THE TIME Dawson heard a sound outside the cave and moved quickly to Jinx's side.

"Jinx!" The word echoed faintly across the meadow. Just as she'd predicted, at least one of the rustlers had come back for her.

"Listen," she whispered as she glanced frantically toward the dark entrance of the cave. "We're on the same side. I can help you."

"On the same side?" Dawson chuckled as he quickly reached into his pocket for his bandanna. "Sorry, but I have to do this," he said as he used the bandanna for a gag, then tied her wrists and ankles with a length of the rope, securing it to his saddle. "If you try to get anyone's attention outside this cave, I will do a lot more than gag you. Understood?"

With her hands tied behind her and her ankles bound she might still be able to move, but she wouldn't get far dragging the saddle before he came back.

She glared at him, those blue eyes flaming with heat, as he picked up his rifle and headed for the mouth of the cave.

The night was clear and cold at this altitude. He slipped from the cave, looking back to make sure no light escaped. It appeared pitch-black inside the opening. The brush hid even that from the meadow. Assured that no one could find the cave without knowing where it was, he made his way down the mountainside, keeping to the blackness of the trees.

The rider had stopped in the middle of the meadow and now sat on his horse, shining his flashlight into the darkness at the edges of the trees. Could he smell the smoke in the air? Dawson didn't think so. At least, he was counting on that.

"Jinx!" the man called again, then seemed to sit listening.

Dawson had stopped behind a tree and now stood stone still, waiting for the rider to make a sound before he moved closer. He knew that if he shot the rustler, the sound alone might bring the others, depending on how far they'd driven the cattle. If this man didn't return tonight, Dawson didn't doubt that they would come looking for him.

As much as Dawson hated rustlers and put them right up there with horse thieves, he didn't like the idea of killing anyone. He'd just as soon let the law handle him. The problem was how to get his cattle back without getting rid of the rustler. Short of shooting someone, he wasn't sure how to do that.

He thought about what Jinx had said right before he gagged her. "We're on the same side." What did that mean? Or had it just been another ploy?

Shoving thoughts of Jinx to the back burner, he concentrated on the problem at hand. One of the rustlers had come back for her. The boyfriend? He thought about her earlier attempt at seduction and wondered just what she'd had to do to get into the rustling ring. That was another thought he didn't want to dwell on too closely—and definitely not right now.

The woman was nothing if not determined. He liked her spunk. The fact that she was cute as hell didn't hurt.

He reminded himself that she'd been trying to steal his cattle—and that if this was the same band of rustlers, which he suspected it had to be, then she and the others had already killed a ranch manager down in Wyoming who'd tried to stop them.

They'd burned down his house after trampling him in the stampeding cattle, which told Dawson that these rustlers were after more than cattle and the money they could get for them. They wanted to terrorize people they felt had more than they did and would take everything—including their lives.

With one rustler hog-tied in the cave and her boyfriend back for her, Dawson had to decide what to do. He didn't doubt for a moment that the man would kill him if he got the chance. But even if Dawson could capture him without it involving gunfire and bringing the other rustlers hightailing it back here, what would he do with him?

No way could he keep track of two prisoners and still go after his cattle. And while he might enjoy leaving them both tied up either in the cave or to a couple of trees, he couldn't be sure they would still be there by the time the sheriff was notified and could get up here to collect them. Not to mention that a grizzly bear or wolves would probably get them both before then.

He wondered if he would have felt this way if one of the rustlers hadn't been a woman and swore under his breath at the thought. The last thing he wanted to do was cut Jinx any slack, since she was one of them.

The contrast between the black trees and the starlit sky was enough that after a moment his eyes adjusted to the darkness. The meadow seemed bathed in a faint eerie light. As he hunkered in the trees, he could make out the cowboy on the horse moving slowly across the open space to the spot where the man had probably last seen Jinx. The rustler was searching the ground, but there was no way he could track her—or Dawson—not with the meadow all torn up from the stampeding cattle.

"Jinx!" the man called again. *"Jinx?"*

How long would this man look for her before he assumed she'd just taken off? Or gotten lost? Or was lying dead somewhere after being crushed by the cattle? Would he come back in the daylight to look for her? Or cut his losses and put all his efforts into getting the stolen cattle to a spot where they could be loaded onto a semitrailer and transported to wherever he planned to sell them?

The rustler kept looking, riding around the perimeter of the meadow. It made Dawson wonder again about the cowboy's relationship with the woman tied up in the cave. Jinx was a pretty young thing, the kind of woman who could definitely get her spurs into a man and take him for a wild ride.

But any man with a lick of sense could see that no man could get a lasso on a woman like her that would hold.

"Jinx!" the rustler called. "If you can hear me, try to be at the rendezvous spot in the morning." He finished riding in a wide circle around the meadow, his flashlight flickering in and out of the trees, then finally going out.

Dawson held his breath, listening, knowing the rustler was listening, as well. Then the rider began to move again through the meadow as if reluctant to leave, heading back the way he'd come. He stopped at the edge of the trees, called out one more time for her, then rode into the darkness of the forest and disappeared.

Hunkered down in the trees, Dawson stayed where he was for a few minutes to make sure the rustler was gone. Then he worked his way back toward the cave and the woman he hoped was still there waiting for him, because he wanted some answers.

SHERIFF MCCALL CRAWFORD kicked off her boots, plopped down next to her husband and put her feet up. It had been a long day and she was thankful to be home. As she settled in, she looked around the room. She loved the house her husband had built for them and this sitting room was her favorite.

A cool breeze scented with summer came in the open windows. She smiled over at Luke. He looked as if he'd had a rough day, as well.

"Any news?" he asked as he glanced over at her.

She shook her head. "Hoyt Chisholm wanted to see me earlier. Apparently Emma's left him. He swears Aggie Wells did something to her."

"Aggie Wells? The missing woman?"

McCall nodded. "I feel sorry for him, but I don't blame Emma for leaving him. If I'd been her, I would have hightailed it out of there the moment I heard about his third wife's body being found and his bolo tie being discovered at the scene."

"What happened to innocent until proven guilty?"

"You think he's innocent?" she asked her husband.

Luke sighed and leaned his head back against the couch cushion. "Admittedly, the evidence against him looks pretty bad."

"There's something about the missing Aggie Wells that is bothering you, isn't there?" she said, sitting up and turning to face him.

He smiled and reached out to caress her cheek. "Isn't it bothering you?"

"Yes! When Emma told me she'd smelled Aggie's perfume at the house, of course I didn't believe her. But this afternoon I got a letter from her. She had apparently mailed it before she left town. She claims Aggie bugged the main house at the ranch. She told me to check the fire alarms and even drew me a picture where I could find them."

"And?" Luke asked with interest.

"And I called the house. Emma is gone, just like Hoyt said. The sons are all staying there, but none of them were back at the house yet. I'm going out there tomorrow and see if there is anything to her story. But what if Emma is telling the truth?"

"You think Aggie kidnapped her?"

"I don't know what to think. Emma is convinced Aggie is behind her own disappearance. Hoyt believes Emma is in danger. If you'd seen his face…"

Her husband pulled her into his arms. "You can't do anything about this until morning. What motive would Aggie have for kidnapping Emma?"

"Maybe she just wants to get rid of her so she can have Hoyt."

"Then why has she gone to so much trouble to make him appear guilty of his other wives' deaths?" her logical husband asked.

McCall groaned. "That's the part I can't figure. Maybe Aggie doesn't know herself what she wants out of this."

"That I find hard to believe. If she went to the

trouble of staging her own disappearance and kidnapping Emma, then she has a plan, you can bet on that."

JINX HAD NO WAY OF TELLING how long Chisholm had been gone. The fire had burned down to only glowing embers. When she looked toward the cave entrance all she saw was darkness. The quiet inside the cave was deafening. It fooled with her sense of time passing.

She'd known Rafe would come back for her. She hadn't been surprised when she'd heard him calling her name. He'd come, she knew, not because he had any real affection for her. He hadn't had a choice. The others didn't trust her. They'd been suspicious of her from the beginning and hadn't wanted her to ride with them.

But Rafe was their leader, though definitely not the brains behind the rustling operation. No, he was more the brawn, a tough ranch hand who'd done some time in the Wyoming pen. The others could push him only so far and she thought they knew it. Her disappearing would make them even more suspicious of her and question Rafe's judgment as well as his position.

Rafe would be worried that they were right. He wouldn't trust her after this. Not unless she could convince him that she'd been captured and had gotten away.

She struggled to free her bonds, giving up when she realized Dawson had made sure she wasn't going anywhere. She froze, listening for a gunshot that would tell her which way the wind was going to blow, so to speak. There was still the chance that Dawson Chisholm was the ringleader and had gone down to meet Rafe and that they would both be coming back up here to decide what to do with her.

Why didn't she believe that scenario any longer? Because Chisholm had been nice to her? Because she'd shared his food? Because she was attracted to him and, on a few scarce moments, liked him?

She cursed herself for telling him she was on his side. She'd taken a gamble based on nothing more than desperation. Normally she depended on her intuition, but with Chisholm she couldn't trust it.

Now he was out there with Rafe and she hadn't a clue what might be happening. Were the two of them at this moment discussing what to do with her? Or was Chisholm about to get himself killed? The thought sent an arrow of panic through her. Did he really think he stood a chance against a man like Rafe Tillman?

Another dire thought came on the heels of the first. She could die in this cave. If Chisholm didn't come back, Rafe would never find her and with her bound and gagged up here—

Jinx started at a sound at the entrance of the cave. She knew someone had entered, but it was too dark to see a thing in that direction. She sensed movement, heard the grate of boot soles on the cave floor approaching her and closed her eyes, bracing herself for the worst.

A moment later she felt a hand touch her arm and let out a startled cry, muted by the gag.

"I'm going to remove your gag," Chisholm whispered next to her. "Don't try to scream or call for help. Your boyfriend is gone."

She opened her eyes, blinked. He was little more than a shadow in the dying firelight. He snapped on a flashlight and laid it on the cave floor, then removed her gag.

She licked her dry lips. "He's not my boyfriend." She hated that her voice broke, that she sounded as frightened as she felt.

Chisholm smiled at that.

What had happened outside the cave? She hadn't heard a shot, but that didn't mean he hadn't killed Rafe. Or that the two weren't in cahoots. Her heart began to pound harder as she looked past him, expecting to see Rafe in the cave entrance. "Where is Rafe?" she finally managed to ask.

"Rafe, huh?" Chisholm said. "So that's your boyfriend's name."

"I told you, he isn't my boyfriend."

He started to untie her ankles, but stopped. She couldn't see his face, but she could feel his fingers brush her tender flesh. His touch was gentle, his fingertips cool and calloused.

She hadn't noticed how calloused his hands were before, and now it took her by surprise. Dawson wasn't one of those ranchers who drove around town in his new truck while someone else worked the place.

Jinx hated that this man had gotten to her. She didn't want to see him get killed, and yet how was she going to keep that from happening when he was determined to go after the rustlers and get his cattle back?

Chapter Five

"A few ground rules before I untie you," Dawson said quietly. "You try anything and I'll hog-tie you and leave you in this cave for the sheriff. And from here on out, I don't want anything but the truth coming from those pretty lips of yours. Where are my cattle?"

She started to speak, but he stopped her with a hand on her arm.

"I'm warning you. Don't lie to me. And I want to know what you meant about us being on the same side."

Jinx met his gaze in the ambient glow of the flashlight. "There is something I need from you first, Chisholm."

He shook his head, looking amused. "Apparently you haven't noticed that you aren't in the best of bargaining positions right now."

Dawson saw the indecision in her expression. She didn't trust him any more than he trusted her.

She met his gaze. Tears shone in those big blue

eyes. "I was only riding with the rustlers so I could get to the head of the rustling ring."

Dawson dropped to his haunches in front of her. "You expect me to believe that?"

"Under normal circumstances, I really wouldn't give a damn one way or the other," she snapped. Her eyes glittered with a sobering rage and, against his better judgment, he did believe her.

"Vengeance? Don't tell me this is because he stole *your* cattle."

"He killed my father."

Dawson frowned. "Your father?"

"The Wyoming ranch manager who was trampled in the stampede. Now do you understand why you have to let me go before it's too late?"

"I'm sorry about your father," he said, softening his words at the pain he saw in her pretty face. "But it's already too late."

She shook her head, clearly refusing to believe him. "Rafe came back for me. If I can catch up to him—"

"Jinx," he said, locking eyes with her. "Do you really think he could ever trust you? No matter what story you came up with, he's going to suspect you. Why didn't you tell me this from the get-go?"

"I would have, but I thought you might be involved. You definitely are coldhearted enough when it comes to your cattle."

He tried not to be insulted. "So you planned to single-handedly take down the rustling ring."

"I still do. Unless you want to help me."

He shook his head. "You're right. I'm coldhearted when it comes to what's mine. You want to get yourself killed, that's your business. I just want my cattle back."

"What about justice?" she demanded.

"Like you said, rustlers seldom get caught, and if they do, they hardly ever get any jail time."

"They *killed* my father."

Dawson nodded. "It's going to be hard to prove murder even if you can tie someone to the head of the rustling ring."

"I'm not worried about proving anything in a court of law." She lifted her chin, that defiant look back in her eyes. "All I need is a few minutes alone with the ringleader."

"Have you ever killed someone in cold blood?" he asked.

She looked away after a moment.

"That's what I thought." He shook his head as he got to his feet again. "But if you're determined to get yourself killed…"

As he started to walk away, she said, "I'll help you get your cattle back. I know where they took them."

The rendezvous point Rafe had mentioned? He stopped, lowered his head, struggling with his own good sense. He'd seen the passion in her eyes. He knew what it felt like to want to avenge a wrong, especially when it was against someone you loved. There was nothing he would have liked more than saving his own father.

He turned slowly.

"You just have to trust me."

"Trust you?" Dawson shook his head. "Let me get this straight. You rode with these rustlers, helping them hit other ranches?"

"This is my first."

"And you have no idea who is behind this rustling ring?"

"I had to gain their trust."

"Just as you're trying to gain mine now," he said with a smile. "Sorry, but I'm not going to let you jeopardize my life and my cattle so you can get yourself killed as part of some crazy revenge scheme."

"I told you. I'll help you get your cattle back, since that's all you care about," she said. "But don't try to stop me from going after what I want. It's a win-win situation."

He no longer had to ask himself how far this woman would go to get what she wanted.

"Chisholm—"

"I don't think you heard me. That cowboy who came after you tonight already suspects you, okay? You think they're going to believe any story you tell them? Hell, they might just shoot you outright the moment they see you."

"I'm willing to take that chance. Well?"

She was as stubborn as he was. He shook his head, angry that she would risk her life. "Let the law handle this. They'll catch these guys."

"Will they? I doubt it. And I know they won't get the person behind the rustlers."

"You don't think Rafe won't spill his guts when he gets arrested? Come on, Jinx, your father wouldn't want you doing this."

"You didn't know my father. You don't know me, for that matter."

He nodded, but he did know her. She reminded him of himself.

"At least I'm risking my life for something I believe in. You're risking yours for *cattle,* the dumbest animals on earth," she said. "So? Do you want your cattle back or not?"

He rubbed the back of his neck, studying her for a long moment. "It's your funeral."

"We have a deal then, Chisholm."

His gaze met hers and held it. Maybe she was a better poker player than he thought, because he was betting his life on the hand she was playing right now.

"Where are my cattle?" he asked as he began to untie her. "And where is the rendezvous point everyone is supposed to meet if something goes wrong?"

AS IT GOT LATE AND THINGS slowed down, Zane talked to a few more of the employees at the hotel. They all said the same thing about Emma McDougal.

"A delightful woman, always cheerful." That was the Emma he'd known at the ranch.

"We are so happy for her. You could tell that the two of them were in love." Zane had to agree from what he'd seen of his father and Emma together.

"Did she ever mention if she had family around here?" he asked each of them and got the same sad shake of the head.

"I think she might have had a family, maybe lost a husband or even a husband and a child. I sensed that about her," one woman from housecleaning told him. "I know she used to talk to her father on the phone. They seemed close."

"Any idea where he lived?" No. "A name?"

"I think I heard her call him Poppy."

As for employment records, Zane was told he would have to wait until the morning and talk to their supervisor. Initially, he was surprised that his father hadn't mentioned Emma had *worked* at the hotel. But then he realized his father wouldn't have found that little tidbit of information important. He probably also knew it might bias his sons if they'd known that from the beginning.

Zane was ashamed that was the case. He was realizing more and more that his father was a better man than he or his brothers were.

"Did she ever mention Caliente Junction, California?" he asked. No. "How about where she was from?" No.

"She never talked about the past."

But everyone had made up a past for Emma, a painful one filled with loss and regret.

He got the same answers from the bartender at closing. "Why does her past matter so much to you?" the young man asked as he wiped down the bar. The place was empty. The man and woman at the bar hadn't even made it until last call for alcohol. Both had been gone when Zane returned to talk to the bartender again.

"Her past is the only way I have of trying to find her," he said.

The bartender looked skeptical. "You're sure you aren't just trying to dig up some dirt on her?"

Zane couldn't deny he'd been worried when his father had rushed into marriage with a woman he clearly knew nothing about. "I like Emma," he said truthfully. "We all do. I just want to find her." That last part might not have been completely true.

If Emma had left his father of her own accord, then he was going to have to tell his father, and he doubted any dirt in Emma's past would be more heartbreaking than her deserting him.

JINX TOLD DAWSON about the rustlers' plan to reach the first corral on the way out of the mountains and bed down the cattle for a night.

The cattle would be tired. If they didn't get them water, food and rest, the rustlers would lose them.

Some would fall behind, and without support to pick up the stragglers, they would be left to die.

He swore under his breath at the thought. "So they are stopping at an old abandoned corral down the mountain for the rest of the night, then moving the cattle farther down tomorrow?"

She nodded. "They had planned to move the herd tomorrow on down to the next abandoned homestead. There's a large corral there for their horses."

"Then the next day, they push them on to the county road and the semitrucks waiting for them," Dawson said. "Where is this rendezvous spot?"

"If any of us got lost or anything happened, we'd meet at one of the corrals."

He nodded. But with her missing, he wondered if the rustlers wouldn't change their plans, try to move things up. They could move the cattle only so far each day without losing most of the herd.

"You realize that once I take my cattle back, your life will be in even more danger," Dawson said as they sat around the small fire he'd built. He'd made them coffee and they now sat next to each other, both staring into the flames. "There will be hell to pay and who do you think they are going to blame?"

"You just worry about getting your cattle back," she said without looking at him. "I can convince Rafe to let me tell his boss what happened," she said into the stony silence.

Dawson shook his head. "You and Rafe are that close?"

She let out an irritated sigh. "If you're asking if Rafe and I are lovers, the answer is no. I did what I had to do to get in with the rustlers, but there are lines I won't cross."

He glanced over at her, wondering if when she'd tried to seduce him earlier she would have crossed that line. He thought there was probably a better chance of finding himself with a gun barrel stuck in his ribs.

"This quest for justice, it won't bring your father back."

"Don't tell me you wouldn't do the same thing if it was your father," she said. "My father was a lot like you, determined not to let them take cattle that didn't even belong to him. It cost him his life."

Dawson rose and walked to the cave entrance. The fire had burned down to embers again, making the back of the cave glow warm with light and heat. But where he'd gone was dark. Starlight bathed the meadow in a shimmering silver.

He heard her come up behind him and tensed for a moment but didn't turn. In that instant, he knew she would have to overpower him. It was the only way he was going to let her go back to the rustlers.

She joined him in the cave opening, the two of them silhouetted against the night. He could make out a sliver of moon over the trees, the pines etched black against cobalt-blue. The air was crisp and fresh and he couldn't remember a time when he'd felt so aware of a woman. The night seemed alive with an electric current that made everything about it more intense.

As he looked over at Jinx, he wondered what it would have been like to have met under other circumstances. She met his gaze. A shudder moved through him and it took all his strength not to pull her into his arms.

"You should try to get a couple hours of sleep," he said as he turned to go back into the cave.

JINX LET OUT THE BREATH she'd been holding. Just moments before, she'd felt a connection to this man…. She shook her head, telling herself that she'd only imagined it. All Chisholm cared about were his damned cattle.

She followed him back into the cave. He seemed almost angry as he tossed her his bedroll. "We leave before daybreak, so you should get some rest. We are definitely going to need the element of surprise."

"I don't want to take your bedroll," she said and held it out to him. He didn't take it. Instead he asked, "So it was just you and your dad?"

Was he testing her? Was it possible he still didn't believe her story? She was too tired to care. She spread the bedroll out in front of the fire and sat down on it, leaning back against the cave wall. "My mother died when I was a baby."

Kindness filled his eyes. "I'm sorry." He sat down next to her. "You've had a lot of death to deal with." He leaned back and she saw exhaustion and something more in his eyes.

She'd heard about his father being arrested for murdering one of his wives. The story had made all the major papers because of who Hoyt Chisholm was. His arrest was one of the reasons she'd talked the rustlers into hitting Chisholm Cattle Company.

"I was fine with just my dad," she said. "I was raised on the ranch, started riding on my own as soon as I could sit a saddle. That life gets in your blood."

"Doesn't it, though," he agreed.

"What about you, Chisholm?"

He smiled. "You already know my story. You got it when you researched my family ranch to steal our cattle."

She didn't deny it, but she was sorry that he'd figured out the part she'd played in all this. Was this any better than him thinking she'd slept with Rafe to get her spot with the rustlers?

Jinx knew his story. With no father in the picture, he and his brothers had been adopted by Hoyt Chisholm. The triplets, Colton, Logan and Zane, had also gotten lucky—Hoyt later adopted them after their mother died in childbirth. All had been young and had needed a home where they wouldn't be separated. Hoyt Chisholm had provided it.

"At least you had your brothers. I was an only child. I did have a great-aunt who used to visit once in a while, though." She laughed softly at the memory. "If anyone influenced my life's decisions, it was Auntie Rose," she said, still smiling at the memories. "She was a rebel, a true outlaw, and she taught me everything I know about surviving in a man's world."

Chisholm shot her an amused look. "You obviously learned well."

Did she sense conflict in him? He'd said all he wanted were his cattle, but she wondered if he was having a hard time letting the rustlers get away—even when she assured him she wasn't going to let that happen.

"About the morning," she said.

"Don't try to talk me out of it."

She just didn't want to get him killed—and she feared she couldn't prevent it if he went after his cattle. "It's your funeral," she said, giving his own words back to him.

He said nothing, but when she looked over at him, she saw his dark eyes lit with amusement and his full sensual mouth turned up in a smile.

The kiss was so unexpected, Jinx gasped. One moment he was smiling at her and the next his lips were on hers. It couldn't have lasted more than an instant, but she felt herself melt into it, drawn to a desire that didn't take her completely by surprise. She'd felt the sparks between them at the front of the cave. Now she knew without a doubt that she hadn't imagined any of it.

He jerked back, looking as surprised as she felt. The next moment he was on his feet. But for that instant she'd seen the chink in his armor—she'd glimpsed the man behind the mule-headed, arrogant cowboy. Her heart beat a little faster because of it.

She said nothing as she watched him pick up his saddle and pour himself the last of the coffee before he headed back toward the cave entrance.

Did he expect Rafe to come back? Or was he just keeping his distance from her?

Chapter Six

Jinx came out of a deathlike sleep. She jerked awake and reached for her gun, only to find it gone. It took her a moment to remember where she was—and with whom.

She blinked, her eyes adjusting to the dim light, to find Chisholm standing over her. She felt such a wave of relief. For a moment she'd thought it was Rafe. Not that she would admit it to Chisholm, but Rafe scared her.

"What is it?"

"Time to go." He was looking at her strangely, giving her the impression that he'd been standing over her for some time watching her sleep. The thought made her heart beat faster.

"You haven't changed your mind, have you?" she asked as she threw off the sleeping bag and got to her feet.

"If you're asking if I trust you, the verdict is still out," he said as he tied up the bedroll and turned to head out of the cave.

"I'm asking if you're going to let me go once we find the rustlers," she said to his retreating backside. There was something in the set of his shoulders that told her the verdict was still out on that, as well.

As she started after him, she noticed that their saddles were gone. She'd slept right through him packing up everything and apparently saddling their horses. Exiting the cave into the clear, cold darkness, she spotted their mounts in the starlight below them on the mountain. Without needing to check her watch, she knew it would be daylight in an hour or so. By then they would have reached the first corral.

Glancing over at Chisholm, she wished there was some way to talk him out of going with her. But she could see by his expression it would take nothing short of death.

Jinx gave only a moment's thought to taking off on her horse and trying to reach the corral before him. That was if she could outrun him. Her horse was fast, but she didn't like the odds, given what she'd seen of the rancher. After all, he'd caught her before and risked life and limb to stop her.

She didn't doubt he would do it again.

Warning Rafe and the rest of them would only get Chisholm killed. She was determined to keep that from happening. But he wasn't making it easy.

She would have to bide her time. All she could hope was that she got lucky and found a way to still get what she desperately needed—the leader of this rustling ring and the man she held responsible for her father's death. She would bring him down—then the others.

"I'm going to need my gun back," she said as they reached the horses.

Chisholm swung up into his saddle and she thought for a moment he hadn't heard her. "You'll get it back after I get my cattle."

"That's a mistake," she said as she mounted her horse. "You're going to need all the help you can get once we find the rustlers."

"Arming you could be an even bigger mistake. There is nothing like a woman bent on revenge." They were close enough she saw the gleam in his dark eyes. He thought she was dangerous. Determination had hardened the lines of his handsome face. But it was no longer just about his cattle. He was mad at himself for kissing her.

EMMA WOKE TO DARKNESS. She wasn't sure at first what had startled her awake until she heard movement and rolled over to find Aggie standing over her.

"What is it?" she cried, hurriedly sitting up.

Aggie hadn't said a word. Nor had she moved. And yet Emma sensed something had happened and was filled with fear at the thought that she might never see Hoyt again. Under the fear was a deep ache that made it hard to breathe. Before Hoyt, she had never known this kind of love.

"What's happened?" she asked, sliding back to rest against the wall. It felt cold and yet solid, and right now she needed solid.

"Hoyt doesn't believe you left him," Aggie said. There was anger and frustration in her voice as she snapped on a flashlight, blinding Emma for a moment. "He seems to think something has happened to you."

Emma tried to hide the pleasure she felt. She'd prayed that Hoyt would know she would never leave him, that she believed in his innocence and would stand by him no matter what.

"Zane has gone to Colorado to try to find you."

She felt tears come to her eyes. Her wonderful stepsons—as tough as she'd been on them, now one of them was looking for her. Her heart swelled. Hoyt *did* know her. He wouldn't give up until he found her—even from jail.

Aggie looked disgusted in the ambient glow from the flashlight.

"This got you up before daylight?" Emma asked as a thought struck her. Had someone called Aggie to let her know about Zane's trip to Colorado? *No,* she thought with a curse. Aggie was probably still listening to everything that happened at the house. The sheriff either hadn't gotten her letter about the listening devices—or hadn't believed her.

"You're going to have to send Hoyt a letter," Aggie said as if the idea had just come to her. "You're going to have to convince him to call off his sons. For your safety——and theirs. Otherwise…"

Emma didn't want to think about the otherwise as Aggie left the room, locking the door behind her. Was she planning on mailing the letter from Denver to make it look as if Emma had gone there? Or somewhere even farther away from Whitehorse, Montana?

It had never crossed her mind that Aggie might have someone helping her. She'd thought the woman had been acting alone. But now she feared Aggie had resources no one knew about, including perhaps someone as fanatical as she was.

THE HUGE MONTANA SKY was getting lighter by the time they neared the abandoned corral. With it just over a rise, Dawson reined in his horse, aware of Jinx beside him. He glanced up at the last of the stars glittering overhead and said a silent prayer, knowing they might need it, since they had no idea what was awaiting them just over this hill.

Dawson could hear the cattle lowing in the predawn. The sound he had grown up with and loved now felt lonely.

He looked over at Jinx and wished to hell he'd left her tied up in the cave. But he knew that might have put her in even more danger if the rustlers went looking for her after he took back his cattle and before he could get help.

As Dawson studied her in the faint light of the

new day, he wished he could change a lot of things. He was about to jeopardize both of their lives. The thought almost made him laugh. Even if he'd left Jinx in the cave, it wouldn't stop her from going after the rustlers and their leader. There was nothing like a woman set on revenge—or justice.

He turned his attention from Jinx to the best way to take the rustlers by surprise. The sky was lightening to the east. It wouldn't be long before dawn. He figured with Jinx missing, the rustlers would be up early—and expecting trouble.

They'd ridden through silvery darkness and now the old Mill Creek place was just over the rise.

"We strike fast," Dawson whispered now as he reached over and tied her hands with the hank of rope again—this time, putting her hands in front of her.

She looked up in surprise.

"I'm just trying to keep them from killing you," he said. "If they think I took you prisoner, they might believe you. I wouldn't bet on it, though." He pulled out his bandanna. His gaze met hers as she leaned toward him so he could tie the gag.

"Last chance to change your mind," he said.

She shook her head. He swore and gagged her.

He knew there was nothing else he could say, and daylight was burning its way up the mountain to the east. If they were going to do this, it had to be now.

"Good luck." He felt his heart pounding in his chest painfully. "I'd tell you to be careful, but…"

She nodded, a smile in her eyes. Then she spurred her horse and took off, as if like him, she feared what he might say. He was hot on her heels as they came up over the rise.

SHERIFF MCCALL CRAWFORD pulled up in front of the main house at Chisholm Cattle Company. It was early, the sun was just coming up off the prairie floor to the east, but she wanted to catch the Chisholms before they went off to do their chores.

As she stepped from her patrol SUV, Marshall Chisholm came out onto the porch. He looked wary. Like all the Chisholm men, he was handsome and exuded confidence. Three of the Chisholm brothers had the coal-black hair and eyes that reflected their Native American ancestry. The other three were blond with blue eyes.

"I'm here about Emma."

"You found her?" Marshall had the mocha coloring, the dark hair and eyes and high cheekbones. There was a gentleness about him that belied his powerful size.

"No, I'm sorry. I take it you haven't heard from her?" McCall said.

He shook his head.

"She sent me a letter. Would you mind if I came inside?"

"You might as well," Marshall said. "My brothers are going to want to hear this."

Three of his brothers were sitting around the kitchen table when she walked in but they rose at the sight of her, all looking wary and worried. Colton and Logan were two of the fraternal triplets, both blond and blue-eyed and just as handsome as the others.

"Is this about Dad?" Colton asked. He'd recently become engaged to one of McCall's deputies, Halley Robinson.

"It's sheriff department business." McCall put a finger to her lips and stepped around the table to look up. The small smoke alarm was right where Emma had said it would be. "If you don't mind, I'd like to speak with all of you outside. I have something in my patrol car I need to show you."

They looked surprised but followed her out of the house. Once they were standing next to her SUV, McCall said, "Where's Zane and Dawson?" Zane was the third of the triplets.

"Dawson's up checking the cattle on summer range," Marshall said. Dawson was the older brother of Marshall and Tanner.

"Zane's gone to find Emma," Logan said. Unlike his brothers, he wore his blond hair long and was the rebel of the family, spending his off time not on horseback but on a motorcycle. "What's going on?"

"Emma left me a message at my office yesterday.

She said that your house is bugged with listening devices."

"That's crazy," Marshall said.

"Maybe not," the sheriff said. "She told me what to look for. Did any of you put up that small smoke alarm hidden on the other side of your kitchen light?"

They all looked at one another. Logan spoke first. "I've never even noticed it before I saw you looking at it. Why would we put it there when Dad installed new smoke alarms last year all through the house in plain sight?"

"Emma believed that Aggie Wells isn't just alive, but that she's been in your house," McCall said. "That she's been eavesdropping on everything that is being said there."

"Are you telling us you agree with Dad, that Aggie Wells might have done something to Emma?" Colton asked as if seeing where this was going.

"I don't know what to believe at this point. But if Emma is right and Aggie Wells is alive and those smoke alarms in there are really listening devices... I know that's a lot of ifs, but that smoke alarm looks like one of the new high-tech listening devices any fool can buy off the internet."

"Well, we're about to find out," Marshall said, turning back toward the house.

McCall caught his arm to stop him. "Wait, if Aggie is listening in on your conversations, what has she heard? Did you mention that Zane had gone to look for Emma?"

Marshall swore.

"We've been staying here at the house, so I would imagine she's heard everything that was said," Colton said. "Including that Zane has gone to Denver to try to find out anything he can about Emma."

The brothers looked as worried as McCall felt.

"These listening devices," Colton said. "Doesn't she have to be nearby with some sort of transmitter?"

McCall shook her head. "The new ones can be accessed through a cell phone or computer. Aggie doesn't even have to be in the area. But I do have an idea. There might be a way to make sure Emma was right about this. We need to disable the one in the kitchen, but we have to make it look like an accident."

"Are you suggesting a little roughhousing between brothers?" Marshall asked.

"Or a knock-down, drag-out fight," McCall said. "Think you can do that?"

They laughed at that. "Not that any of us ever fight. Then what?" Colton asked.

"If you all do most of your talking in the kitchen in the morning, if it is a listening device and if Aggie is alive and listening, then she's going to want to come and fix it. You'll just have to make sure she knows when all of you will be out of the house for a length of time. Emma said she found several other small smoke alarms in the house." She told them the locations.

"So she can still hear us if we're in the house," Colton said with a nod.

"Do you think she's hurt Emma?" Logan asked, sounding upset.

McCall hoped not. "If Aggie staged her own disappearance hoping to make Hoyt look guilty of her murder, then with Hoyt in jail, I believe she won't hurt Emma. Once he's out…"

"If she wants to frame him for Emma's murder, he has to be out of jail," Logan agreed.

"But Dad is trying to make bail. He's desperate to find Emma," Marshall said. "His new lawyer thinks he might be able to get him out by the weekend. He's pulling every string possible, including going to the governor."

"I doubt telling our father what's going on would make him slow down that process," Marshall said. "If anything, he will try to get out sooner."

"So we don't tell him," Logan said.

"If you're right, then Aggie is going to be curious about what you showed us in your patrol car," Colton said. "Is it anything we might want to argue about?"

The sheriff smiled. "More evidence against your father and a warning for you Chisholms not to interfere in my investigation. Is that sufficient?"

"Hell, we've never needed a reason to fight,"

Logan said. "You have to find Emma. If something happens to her…"

"Let's see if we can't draw out whoever installed these smoke alarms and start from there," McCall said. "That's *if* the smoke alarm is a high-tech listening device. I don't need to tell you that looking for Emma if Aggie has her in this part of Montana would be like looking for a needle in a haystack. My deputies are already looking for Aggie. Once you have the smoke alarm disabled, bring it to me. If it is a listening device, then we'll set the trap and see what falls into it."

EARLY-MORNING MIST HUNG in the air as Dawson rode over the rise after Jinx. The minute he topped the hill, he saw the corral below bathed in the faint light of dawn and heard the bawling cattle and knew what the rustlers had done.

The rustlers had felt pressured and had been forced to leave some of the calves behind that couldn't go any farther.

Dawson had his rifle drawn, ready for the rustlers to show. But nothing but the calves in the corral moved in the abandoned ranch yard. No guard. The rustlers had been expecting trouble. Only the corrals still stood, the house nothing more than a decaying foundation of charred small stones and mortar after an apparent fire.

There was a chill in the air, a dampness from the

morning dew that glistened on the grass. The calves bawled loudly as he and Jinx rode in. Dawson cursed the rustlers as he reined in.

Jinx had stopped a few yards from the corral and now sat looking despondent. Like him, she had to realize that her boyfriend Rafe was more than a little suspicious of her. The rustlers must have moved the cattle farther east, closer to where the semitrailers would be picking them up for quick sale to some crooked cattle buyer.

He swung down off his horse and walked over to untie her hands. As she took off the bandanna gag, even in the dim light, he saw her defeat.

"How far is it to the next corral they planned to use?" he asked. "I'll herd these cattle down to it today." It would be slower going, but he didn't want to leave them here.

As he started over to open the gate, she said, "They'll be expecting you to do that."

"I know," he said without turning around. "But I can't leave these calves here like this."

Dawson turned to look at her. She wanted to go after the rustlers, catch up with them. She didn't want to herd a bunch of calves down to the next corral.

"I can't stop you from leaving," he said, meeting her gaze. "It would probably be better that way. If they catch you riding with me…"

He could see from her expression that his offer had taken her by surprise. She actually looked at a loss for words. He wasn't just offering to let her go. He'd just told her he trusted her.

You're a damned fool.

Probably, he admitted. She could ride out, warn the rustlers and they would get away with as many cattle as they could herd to the truck. But if she had any chance of survival, given her determination to bring down this rustling ring, then she had to get as far away from him as possible.

He waited for her to overcome her initial surprise and take off like a shot.

But she surprised him.

"I'll ride with you as far as the next corral," Jinx said as she swung down from her horse and, taking off her straw hat, slipped through the corral fence to wave it in the air. The calves began to move toward the open gate.

She was going to help him move the calves down to their mothers? Didn't she realize how dangerous that was going to be if the rustlers were waiting in ambush?

He felt a hitch in his chest. As much as she wanted justice, she couldn't chance that Rafe would send a couple of his men back up this way to check out whatever story she came up with. She was worried about saving him.

The last thing Dawson wanted was that. The woman was neck deep in a rustling ring. Whatever her good intentions, he suspected she'd been the one to target his ranch. Jinx was far from an innocent in all this and it aggravated him that he'd let her get to him.

"You sure about this?" he said as she turned away from him.

She let out a laugh as she swung up into her saddle and began to move the cattle east toward the rising sun. "I'm sure I'm a damned fool."

He knew the feeling. As he spurred his horse and they began to move the calves down the mountain in search of their mothers, he reminded himself that he hadn't changed Jinx's mind about going after the leader of the rustlers. He'd only postponed the inevitable.

He supposed he should be glad of that. Did he really think it possible to get her to come to her senses?

As they began to move the calves toward the next abandoned corral and hopefully their anxious mothers, he couldn't help watching Jinx. She was as good in the saddle rounding up cows as any cattleman he'd known.

He reminded himself that once they reached the next corral she'd be riding off into the sunset and not even looking back. She was a woman on a quest and a man didn't want to get in the way of a woman like that.

Keep your distance from this woman.

But the warning fell on deaf ears.

As they topped a rise, he looked out across the wild country. He knew the next corral wasn't far, from what Jinx had told him. Up here in this part of Montana there were a lot of abandoned old ranch places. It was big country, inhospitable a large part of the year with blizzards, howling wind that brought in dangerous storms and below-zero temperatures in the winter, and blazing heat, mosquitoes the size of bats and stunning sunsets all the other months.

The hardest part for some was the loneliness. Ranches were few and far between, the sky up here vast, the land seeming to go on forever without another living soul for miles. It took a special kind of person to appreciate it.

Dawson thought of Emma and his dad and felt a heart-wrenching ache. He'd actually thought his father had finally found the perfect wife for him.

As he looked over at Jinx, he saw that she had reined in and was looking out across the country with a kind of awe. She had removed her straw hat to catch some of the breeze that ruffled her blond hair. Her face was lightly tanned, her eyes the same blue as the big sky that spread out before them.

As hard as he tried not to, he lost a little piece of his heart.

Chapter Seven

Aggie returned with paper and pen—and of course a gun. She dropped the paper and pen onto the mattress and leaned against the wall, the gun in her hand.

While Aggie had been gone, Emma had used the buckets in the closet. Just washing her face and cleaning up a little made her feel stronger.

"I'm going to need some fresh clothing," Emma said from where she'd been standing and peering out a space between the boarded-up window. "I assume you removed my clothing from the house and still have it."

She'd realized that if Aggie had gotten rid of her belongings, then she wasn't planning on letting Emma live.

Aggie studied her for a moment without answering, making Emma's heart pound. Was she upset that Emma had asked for a change of clothing? Or did she realize as Emma did, that if she admitted to getting rid of Emma's things, then they would both know what her plans were?

Emma so far had been the perfect prisoner, not asking for anything, not trying to escape. She'd thought it better to bide her time.

But she needed fresh clothing and she was tired of pretending to be the perfect prisoner. However this ended, Emma wasn't about to go down in a cowardly fashion if she could help it.

"Write the letter and I'll get you some of your clothes," Aggie said.

Emma glanced toward the paper and pen on the mattress, relieved to hear that Aggie hadn't gotten rid of her things. That had to mean something.

Unless the woman was lying. That was always a possibility.

But Emma had little choice but to go along. "You left a note at the house." She shifted her gaze to Aggie. "I don't remember writing it."

"You didn't. I did."

She cocked a brow. "Aren't you afraid someone will check the handwriting and realize it isn't mine?"

Aggie laughed. "How long have you been in that house? Two months? I really doubt any of your stepsons would know your handwriting. Anyway, the note I left for you at the house was sloppy, hurried as if you were upset. I also made it short and sweet. Now, quit stalling."

Emma walked over to the mattress, sat down on the edge and picked up the paper and pen.

"Here, you can use the tray to write on," Aggie

said, sliding it over to her with her foot. "Start by apologizing for running out on Hoyt." She smiled. "That is what you would do, isn't it? Then tell them you are afraid for your life."

At least that part Emma would write honestly.

"Now write, 'I'm having a friend drop this off at the house.'" She lifted a brow. "You can't really say that Aggie will be dropping it off when no one is home, now, can you?"

So that was how she planned to get the letter to Chisholm Cattle Company quickly. Emma felt better already. Aggie didn't have an accomplice. She was all alone in this. That definitely narrowed the odds— even with Aggie holding the gun.

"EMMA WAS DELIGHTFUL," the fiftysomething male supervisor at the hotel told Zane when they met that morning. "I hated to lose her. Everyone liked her."

"That's what I've heard. I need to find her." He filled the man in on what he knew so far about Emma's disappearance, including the fact that she might be in danger, something he thought very likely after his conversation with his brother Marshall first thing this morning.

He still couldn't believe that the house had apparently been bugged and that even the sheriff was beginning to consider that Aggie Wells wasn't just alive, but that she might have faked her disappearance and taken Emma.

"Did she ever mention family?" he asked the supervisor.

The man shook his head, visibly upset by the news about Emma. "She had a father out in California. I believe they were close, but other than that…"

"Did she mention his name?"

"Sorry. Emma wasn't one to talk about herself."

"She didn't get any mail here?"

"Not that I know of."

"Do you know where she lived?" Zane asked.

"She had an apartment just down the street from here."

Zane glanced toward the front door and the street beyond it. "This is a pretty pricey neighborhood."

"I got the feeling she was careful with her money."

Was it possible she'd come from money? Or married it? Or was just careful with what she made?

She could have been divorced or widowed. Zane swore under his breath; there was no way of knowing. When he'd gone on the internet, he hadn't been able to find an Emma McDougal that matched her age.

"She was like family here at the hotel," the supervisor said.

And if she really had left on her own accord, she would have come back here, Zane thought. Clearly she could have gotten her old job back.

Letters. He thought of the note Emma had allegedly left. After talking to his brother Marshall this morning, he realized there was a chance she either hadn't left it or had been forced to write it.

"You wouldn't happen to still have anything that Emma had written?" he asked. "She left a note, but we suspect it wasn't her handwriting."

"As a matter of fact, I have her employment application. We keep those on file for five years." He went into the office and returned a moment later with a copy for Zane. "You don't see penmanship like this anymore. These kids and their texting—their handwriting is atrocious. I could show you applications that are barely legible."

Zane stared down at Emma's perfect script. There was no way she'd written the note left at the house. Under former employment, the line was blank. The address line was also blank.

"There isn't much on this application," he noted.

The man shook his head. "She'd just gotten to town, didn't have an apartment yet, no past experience, but there was something about her, you know?"

Zane thought he did. He thanked the supervisor.

"When you find Emma, will you tell her that we all miss her?"

"I will," Zane said, aware that Hoyt Chisholm wasn't the only man who'd fallen for Emma at the Denver hotel.

THE SUN ROSE HIGHER, taking the chill out of the mountain air, but Jinx felt little of the warmth. When she'd seen the calves in the corral, she'd known. Rafe wasn't taking any chances. He'd had his men leave the weaker calves that had been slowing them down. He was spooked, which meant he was suspicious of her.

She leaned back in the saddle to stretch her spine. Huge cumulus clouds floated in the sea of brilliant blue over the tops of the pines. The air up here felt so clean she swore it hurt to breathe. She was tired but Dawson, she noted as she glanced over at him, was exhausted. How much longer could he keep going without any sleep? She knew he hadn't gotten any last night.

As an old homestead cabin came into view, she saw Dawson rein in. Like her, he must have spotted the small creek nearby and the meadow of grass. They could push the calves only so hard. It had been slow going and they hadn't made much headway, but she also didn't think they'd left any strays for the wolves and grizzlies to eat.

"We have to stop," he said as she rode over to him. He looked as if he expected an argument from her. He knew how badly she wanted the leader of the rustling ring. So much she could taste it. But she couldn't leave him and the calves. She figured he was counting on that.

Rafe would be pushing the cattle down to the next corral, but he couldn't move up the delivery date because he would have no way to contact the truck drivers with no cell phone service for miles around.

There was time, she told herself as she swung down from her saddle. The calves had already found the creek. She headed for the old cabin. It looked as if it had been used by ranchers who brought their cattle up to summer range, maybe even the Chisholms, though not Dawson. He apparently liked the cave better.

"You can catch up to the herd if you leave now," Dawson said behind her. "I don't want you staying for the wrong reasons." She didn't turn, didn't answer. Rafe would be pushing the cattle toward the last corral, afraid something was amiss with her disappearance. She figured that meant he wouldn't be doubling back again to look for her—or anyone else.

Too bad that wasn't the real reason she was staying here.

"Jinx," Dawson said behind her. There was a softness to his voice as light as a caress. She turned around to face him, saw his expression and told herself she should have taken his advice and ridden out before she got in any deeper.

"Looks like things got rough," McCall said in her office. Marshall had brought her what was left of the listening device after the brothers had put on the fight at the kitchen table. "It's not a smoke alarm. It appears to be some sort of listening device, just as Emma suspected."

Marshall nodded. "She didn't bail on my father, did she?"

McCall studied the pieces he'd brought her. She was beginning to believe more and more that Emma had been right about a lot of things.

"Now what?" he asked.

"We have to assume whoever put this in the kitchen will have heard the fight up until the point where the device was destroyed," the sheriff said. "With luck, that person will wait until he or she is sure all of you are away from the house and then try to replace it."

He smiled, obviously noticing the way she was trying not to say Aggie's name. "Leaving yourself open just in case it isn't Aggie?"

"Just trying not to jump to conclusions."

He nodded. "I checked the house. There are at least two more of these things, one in the living room and another in my dad and Emma's bedroom, just as you said she told you in the letter."

McCall could see how angry he was. "We have to keep our cool," she warned. "If she gets any hint that we're onto her…"

"I know. We need her to lead us to Emma—if she has her."

"Have you heard anything from Zane?"

"He called this morning in the middle of the fight. I called him back from my cell phone away from the house and told him what was going on here," Marshall said. "He's flying to some place in California today, the last address he could find for Emma. I told him to keep looking for her—just in case we're wrong and Emma really did leave. I guess we're covering all our bets."

"Didn't you say your brother Dawson went to check on your cattle up on summer range?"

"Yeah." Marshall frowned. "I got the feeling he'd be gone for a couple of days at least. I don't think we need to worry about him showing up unexpectedly. My brothers and I were talking. We have some new fence we started putting in before Dad was arrested. It's up in the north forty far enough that we wouldn't be coming back to the ranch until late."

"That sounds good. We want her to know you'll be gone for a while. I'll take it from there," the sheriff said.

"You sure you won't need any help?" Marshall asked.

McCall smiled. "Thanks, but I think I can handle it." She knew that all the brothers would be there in a heartbeat if they thought they were needed. She liked the Chisholm men. They were all gallant, all loyal to family.

She thought of her newest deputy, Halley

Robinson, and her fiancé, Colton Chisholm. They made a cute couple. Halley made a darn good deputy. McCall was happy for her and hoped Emma's situation had a happy ending, as well.

"Set it up for tomorrow," she said, afraid to put it off.

Marshall nodded. "Dad said Emma swore she smelled the woman's perfume in the house several times. The last time he didn't believe her. That's really weighing on him right now. He's convinced that not only is Aggie alive but that she might have already hurt Emma. He is doing everything possible to get out on bail. I know he has a call in to the governor."

"Hopefully this will all be over by tomorrow," the sheriff said. If Aggie showed up, McCall was just praying she would lead her to Emma. If Emma was still alive.

THE LOOK IN DAWSON'S DARK EYES spurred Jinx's heartbeat into a gallop.

"Jinx," he said again, the soft timbre of his voice melting her resolve. She watched him yank his Stetson from his head and rake his fingers through his thick black hair. His expression was one of both desperation and desire.

She felt the same stir in her. "Chisholm..." She said his last name as if that could stop him.

It didn't.

In two long strides he closed the distance between them, wrapping his arms around her, dragging her to him, his mouth dropping to hers, stealing her breath, making her heart drum in her chest. She looped her arms around his neck, holding on tight as if in a fierce gale.

"What if Rafe comes back?" she said when he let her come up for breath.

"I don't give a damn about Rafe," he said as his mouth hovered over her lips. And then he was kissing her again, deepening the kiss.

Desire shot through her veins, hot and sweet. She told herself this was a mistake, but she no longer believed that as Dawson cupped her jean-clad bottom and lifted her against him. His mouth dropped from hers and trailed along her jaw to her throat to the tops of her breasts. She felt the heat of his breath, his mouth, as he ferreted one rock-hard nipple from her bra, then another.

With a cry, she arched against him and he lifted her higher, pressing her against the sun-warmed wood of the cabin as he peeled back her shirt, her bra, and found bare skin.

They never made it inside the cabin. As the sun rose high above the pines and clouds drifted past in the endless sea of blue overhead, they made love on their discarded clothing spread across the summer grass as the calves rested in the shade of the trees along the creek and the breeze stirred the leaves on the cottonwoods overhead.

Chapter Eight

The plane banked, giving Zane a view of manicured golf courses, red tiled roofs and shimmering aquamarine swimming pools. After landing in Palm Springs, he rented a car and headed south toward the Salton Sea.

Caliente Junction was pretty much as he'd expected. A convenience store with lots of bars on the windows, a gas station, a boarded-up Mexican food place and several more empty buildings.

He could see what looked like a couple of houses behind the convenience store, small stucco houses sitting out in the middle of the desert. But he had little hope that the address Emma had used was anything more than one she'd pulled out of her hat.

Parking in front of the store, he got out and went inside. He was betting that Emma had some reason for wanting to hide her past and that was why she hadn't shared it with Hoyt.

A bell jangled over the door and he was hit with the rich wonderful scent of homemade tamales. His stomach growled.

An elderly Latino woman appeared behind the counter. "Can I help you?"

"I sure hope so." Zane pulled out the photograph he had of a smiling Emma McDougal Chisholm. "Do you recognize this woman?"

She barely glanced at the photo before asking, "What has she done?"

"She's missing and I'm trying to find her. Her last known address was Caliente Junction."

"Why do you want her? Are you a cop?"

He shook his head. "She's my stepmother. My father is worried something has happened to her. So am I."

The woman studied him for a moment. "You need to talk to Alonzo."

When she didn't say more, he asked, "Where do I find this Alonzo?"

She pointed toward the back of the building. "Last house at the end of the road. You can't miss his truck parked outside. It's blue."

The truck was a lot of blues, a monster vehicle with huge tires and a body that looked as if it had been pieced together by Frankenstein during his "blue" period. Zane parked and walked up to the door. It opened before he could knock.

"Yes?" the large elderly Latino man asked suspiciously. Alonzo was wearing baggy shorts and a huge faded Grateful Dead T-shirt. His feet were bare and it was impossible to tell his age. But if Zane had to guess, it would be late seventies.

He gave Zane the once-over. Zane had wisely left his Stetson at home even though he felt half-naked without his hat. No way was he going anywhere without his boots and jeans, though, so he wore them and a Western shirt, which back home would have been standard ranchman's wear. He had fit right in back in Denver.

Now, though, he felt overdressed. "I just spoke with the woman at the store. She suggested I talk to you. I'm looking for Emma." He handed the man the photo. "I'm not a cop or a bill collector. Emma is my stepmother. I'm afraid she might be in some kind of trouble."

"Your *stepmother?*" The old man sounded disbelieving and for the first time, Zane thought he might be at the right place.

"My dad recently married her."

"Your *dad?*"

But he was getting tired of the echo. "Hoyt Chisholm of Chisholm Cattle Company out of Whitehorse, Montana."

The man laughed. "So Emma really did marry a cowboy? Come in," he said, pushing the door open wide and stepping back. As Zane entered, Alonzo said, "What's this about Emma being in trouble, though? If anyone can take care of herself, it's our Emma McDougal."

DAWSON LAY ON HIS BACK staring up at the sky overhead. Not since his childhood could he remember watching clouds float by on a summer day and feeling so content. He breathed in the sweet scent of the crushed grass beneath him. It mingled with the scent of the woman next to him.

He never wanted to leave here, didn't even want to get up. Right now he would have let the rustlers take the cattle. All that mattered was being here with this woman on this summer day because he knew it couldn't last.

Jinx lay beside him, looking up at the expanse of blue sky dotted with big white clouds. There was a small smile on her lips, a softness to her expression that made him smile as well. The breeze ruffled her short blond curls and he felt an ache for her, a longing. There were some women you could never have, not in a way that promised they would always be there. Jinx was one of them.

"I can't let you go after the rustlers," he said, speaking the fear in his heart.

She turned her head slowly toward him. "Please don't, Dawson."

Dawson. Not Chisholm. He liked the sound of his name on her lips. Hell, he liked her lips on him.

He pushed himself up on one elbow and laid an arm over her warm stomach. Her soft skin spurred another jolt of desire that burned through him like an out-of-control wildfire. He knew that if he had a lifetime, he would never get enough of this woman, this capable, stubborn, determined woman who didn't think she needed anyone.

Well, getting the leader of the rustling ring was one thing he couldn't let her do alone. "Jinx—"

She slid out of his hold, picking up her jeans from the ground as she did. Her panties were still inside the jeans. She moved a few feet away and pulled on both before turning back to him.

He was sitting on the ground, his gaze on her. "You're still determined to go after him alone, aren't you?"

She reached for her Western shirt lying on the ground next to him. He grabbed her wrist, met her gaze, and then slowly let go. "I have to finish what I started."

"Let me help you get him," he said.

"No." She shook her head, the look in her eye warning him not to bother arguing with her about this.

He nodded, chewing at his cheek as he tried to stem his anger. And his hurt. "What about this?" He motioned to the crushed grass, the scent of the two of them still lingering, the memory of the feel of her still fresh on his skin.

Jinx looked into his eyes and said the only thing she could. "It was a mistake." She wanted to take back the words the instant they left her lips. She saw the hurt in Dawson's eyes, but she knew that the one thing she couldn't risk was this man's life.

This was her crazy crusade for justice, a promise she'd made her father as she stood over his casket. She had to do this, but she wouldn't let Dawson get any more involved than he already was.

"I've come too far to stop now," she said, the words like gravel in her mouth as Dawson rose and began to dress, his movements hasty with anger. "It's something I have to do on my own."

"You go back to Rafe alone and you're a dead woman."

"Thanks for the vote of confidence," she snapped. "This is something I have to do. Alone, because that is the only way I can get near the man behind these rustlers. I thought you knew that."

"Knowing it is one thing. Accepting it..." He shook his head.

"I know how dangerous this is." Her voice broke. Dawson Chisholm was another danger, one she hadn't planned on, one she couldn't regret either. But now she had him to worry about and she was desperate to see that nothing happened to him because of her.

"I should have ridden out this morning," she

said, pushing her straw hat down over her tangled blond hair.

"Why didn't you?" he asked, his gaze locking with hers.

She could still smell him on her, still feel his phantom touch on her flesh. "I'll ride with you as far as the next corral. After that, you just concern yourself with your cattle." She turned and headed for her horse.

IT TOOK ALL OF HIS STRENGTH not to go after her and pull her into his arms again. But Dawson knew if he did, he wouldn't be able to let her go. Hell, he'd hog-tie her, whatever he had to do to keep her safe, and she would hate him for it until the day she died.

One look at her and he realized short of taking her prisoner again, there would be no keeping this woman from doing what she'd set out to do from the beginning.

Just as he'd felt about the first woman he'd loved.

The reminder sent an arrow of pain through him. Jinx had nailed it when she'd said there'd been a woman in his life who had been taken from him. Only, Jinx had thought the woman had been taken by another man. He'd lost her nonetheless and he still felt the pain of that loss.

And now he'd met another headstrong woman who was determined to get herself killed. He rose and quickly dressed.

As he swung up in his saddle, she said, "I need you to let me finish this, Dawson."

"Could I stop you?" He shook his head, furious with himself for letting this woman get to him. And she had. Maybe from the moment he'd tackled her thinking she was one of the rustlers. Maybe in the firelight of the cave. But she'd gotten to him. He thought now how apt her name was.

"I've already tangled with one headstrong woman who wouldn't listen to reason when it came to her welfare," he said. "I'm not up to trying to corral another one."

Anger flared in her eyes like a blue flame. "I'm not one of your cattle, Chisholm. I don't need herding—or corralling. I'm my own woman."

"You don't have to tell me that," he said. "I get it. And you're right. This *was* a mistake." With that he reined his horse around and rode down to the creek to get his cattle. He didn't look back. He couldn't. He wasn't letting another dangerous woman get her spurs in him—at least not any deeper than Jinx already had.

MCCALL REALIZED that telling her husband her plan had been a mistake.

"I don't like this," Luke said. "If you're right and Aggie Wells is alive and has Emma, then I shouldn't have to tell you how dangerous she is."

"I'm the sheriff," she said with exasperation. "Forget for a moment that I'm your wife."

"I never forget you're my wife. And I thank my lucky stars." He took her shoulders in his big hands and drew her closer. He had stopped by the sheriff's department on his way to work and now the two of them stood in the middle of her office, the door closed. "I just don't like you being out there alone without backup."

"I'll have backup on the roads in and out of Chisholm Cattle Company. I'll radio if I need help, but I think I can handle one woman."

"Are you sure that's all you're going to have to handle?" he asked. "You're that sure she's working alone?"

The question took her by surprise and it shouldn't have. If Aggie had abandoned her car out by the highway, had someone picked her up? Or had she already arranged for another vehicle that she simply got in and drove away?

"Uh-huh," Luke said. "You're convinced she has been working alone. What if you're wrong?"

"If it turns out she has a small army at her disposal, I will call for backup." She smiled at her husband. Touched that he was worried about her and a little concerned.

"How's your grandmother?" he asked out of the blue.

"Pepper?" McCall hadn't seen much of her lately.

They'd both been busy. "Last time I talked to her, she and Hunt were settling in nicely. She loves having all her grandchildren on the ranch. They're building houses all over the place out there. Why are you asking about her?"

"Because she called me. She's worried about you. She thinks you work too hard. She wants us to come out for supper tomorrow. She also wonders when we're going to have a baby."

McCall quirked a brow. "*She* wonders?"

"She's also worried that you might not be around tomorrow for supper," he said, his gaze locked with hers.

McCall laughed and leaned in to kiss her husband. "Well, you can tell Grandmother or anyone else who's wondering that we'll be there tomorrow night."

He looked skeptical.

"And you can tell whoever else is interested that I think we should have a baby."

"Don't fool with me, McCall Winchester Crawford."

She chuckled. "Let's make a baby tonight."

He broke into a huge smile and pulled her to him, holding her as if he never wanted to let her go.

McCall was a little surprised at how worried he was. They were both in law enforcement, Luke a game warden trained just like she had been when it came to criminals. Often they ended up working together because of the shortage of law enforcement in this part of Montana.

He knew what her job entailed. It was strange that this case in particular had him so worried. Or did it have more to do with him wanting to have a baby?

Either way, it made her more anxious than she wanted to admit. If Aggie Wells was alive, then there was a good chance she had come unhinged. Those were the scariest criminals to confront and apprehend because you never knew what they would do.

McCall knew that was what had her husband worried. He didn't like the idea of her alone in an empty ranch house with a crazy woman. McCall wasn't that excited about it either.

"Ask my grandmother if there is anything I can bring for supper tomorrow night," she said later, trying to reassure them both as she gave him a conspiratorial wink. "By then with any luck, I'll already be pregnant."

EMMA THOUGHT FRANTICALLY about what she could say in the letter to let her stepsons know that she was being held captive by Aggie Wells.

But with Aggie watching over her shoulder with a gun pointed at her, there was little chance of sending a message.

"Tell them to leave you alone, that marrying Hoyt was a mistake and that you don't intend to ever see them again," Aggie ordered.

Emma felt her eyes tear at the thought that she might not see her stepsons again, or Hoyt for that matter. Her heart broke at the thought. She couldn't bear to think that he might believe the words in the letter. Wouldn't he know it was a lie? Didn't he realize how much she loved him?

But she wouldn't be the first wife he believed had left him and, given his terrible luck with wives… or as one local called it, the Chisholm Curse, he might believe the words in the letter, and so might her stepsons.

It was actually the Aggie Wells curse, Emma thought as she wrote what the woman dictated. Aggie might deny that she was behind Hoyt's bad luck with wives since the first one had accidentally drowned, but Emma didn't believe it.

"There," she said as she finished.

"Sign it, Emma. Nothing more."

She did and handed the paper to Aggie.

"The pen, too."

Emma gave her an impatient look. "Did you think I was going to use the pen to break out of here? Or maybe carve it into a shank to use as a weapon?"

"I wouldn't be surprised," Aggie said as she took it. "You must be getting tired of sandwiches, but that's all we're going to have to eat for a while."

"Aggie, how long are we going to do this?"

The woman had stopped at the door. She had the

pen and paper in one gloved hand, the gun in the other. "Do what?"

"Stay here like this?"

"As long as it takes," Aggie said and stepped out, locking the door behind her.

IT WAS A LONG SLOW RIDE to the next corral. The sun made a wide arc through the big Montana sky and had finally dropped over the horizon to the west, leaving streaks of color through the pines.

Farther to the north, though, a bank of dark clouds hunkered on the horizon in what could amount to a thunderstorm before the day was over.

Dawson hadn't said a word since they'd left the cabin. The only sound was the bawling of the calves and the occasional cry of a hawk in the sky over the towering pines as dusk settled in around them.

Jinx was sorry she'd told him that making love with him had been a mistake, but she figured he realized that now. It had been too intimate and she suspected it had left them both feeling vulnerable. They were vulnerable enough with a band of rustlers on the loose.

She wasn't sure Dawson realized how dangerous these men were, but she knew firsthand. The thought of her father lying in the dirt— She felt tears burn her eyes and quickly wiped them away. First she would take down the head of the rustling ring and the rustlers, then she would deal with her loss and let herself grieve.

Going after the rustlers and their leader had been the only way she could cope. She knew it wouldn't bring her father back, that it was dangerous, even stupid, but at least it was something she could do. Getting justice wouldn't fill the hole her father's death had left inside her. But it would maybe give her a little peace.

Ahead, she recognized a rocky bluff that sat high above a section of abandoned ranch. The calves had smelled water and were now bursting through the trees and into the open to get to it.

They both had reined in as they spotted the corral. It was empty.

For a moment neither of them moved as if taking this in and what it meant. Rafe and the others had moved the cattle out already. Or had never stopped here to start with.

"What the hell?" Dawson said, glancing over at her before he spurred his horse and rode down to the ranch. What was left of a small old cabin stood against a hillside. In front of it sat a cobbled rock wishing well. A frayed piece of rope hung from the well cover.

Jinx watched it move restlessly in the breeze as she tried to imagine the family who had lived here rather than think about Rafe. The ground was trampled from where the cows had been driven away.

Rafe was more than suspicious of her. He was running scared.

Dawson had reined in his horse at the edge of the empty corral. Past him the land stretched out into the rolling prairie and the dark horizon. From here on out, there would be no trees or mountains to hide in. Unless they traveled at night, they would be in open country—country where someone could see them coming for miles.

As she looked across it, Jinx thought she saw dust rising on the horizon. The cattle herd? They'd never be able to catch it unless they left the calves here and rode hard. Then what?

Suddenly it seemed too quiet even with the bawling calves. Jinx felt the hair rise on the back of her neck. "Dawson!"

But before she could warn him, the sound of a rifle shot filled the air.

Chapter Nine

As Jinx raced down into the ranch yard, she saw Dawson flinch at the crack of the rifle. He reached for his own rifle but even as he did, she knew he was hit. A dark crimson splotch bloomed on his left shoulder.

"Get down!" he yelled as he dived from his horse.

Jinx felt as if everything was moving too fast. She bailed off her horse, diving behind the crumbling rock of the old well as another shot rang out. She couldn't see Dawson, could hardly hear with her heart in her throat and her pulse a war drum.

Another shot, then another. She and Dawson should have expected an ambush, been ready for it. But the ranch yard had seemed so deserted with the cattle gone.

She blamed herself. She knew Rafe had been leery of letting her ride with them from the first. When he hadn't been able to find her, he'd left someone to make sure she didn't turn up—just as Dawson had said.

She thought of her father. She'd been so hell-bent on vengeance, but Dawson was right. Her father wouldn't have wanted this.

"Let God settle the debt in his own time," her father used to say. "Don't think he isn't keeping track."

Tears welled in her eyes and her chest ached with regret and grief. If she'd gotten Dawson killed...

Suddenly she was aware of the eerie quiet again. Not a breath of air moved. She could see the calves down at the creek but they, too, had fallen silent. Somewhere in the distance she heard the song of a meadowlark, then everything fell silent again.

Jinx stayed down, afraid to move, afraid to breathe. If only Dawson had given her back her gun.

She heard the crunch of a boot sole on the dirt, then another. She looked around for anything she could use as a weapon. There was nothing.

A shadow fell over her. With dread, she looked up to see Rafe standing above her, his gun barrel pointed at her head.

OVER HOMEMADE TAMALES, beans and rice, Alonzo told Zane about Emma.

"I was the one who found her," he said proudly.

"Found her?"

He nodded. "It was the middle of the night. I'd been down to the bar at the Salton Sea marina and was coming home. It is a miracle that I saw her." He crossed himself. *"La voluntad de Dios.* It was truly God's will," he translated. "I was driving along and boom! I blew a tire."

Zane was wondering when he was going to get to Emma. So far he couldn't imagine what about a night of drinking, then a flat tire, could be a miracle or had to do with Emma.

"I get out of my truck and realize my spare tire is flat," Alonzo said. "I was thinking what a terrible night it had been." He leaned toward Zane confidentially. "You see, I knew that when I got home Maria was going to be very upset with me. Maria was my wife of fifty-five wonderful years." He crossed himself again and said what Zane took to be a silent prayer.

"Emma," Zane reminded the man.

Alonzo laughed and passed him more tamales. Clearly this was a story he had told many times and with obvious relish.

"So I leave the truck and start to walk and all of a sudden—" his dark eyes lit up and a huge smile formed in his wrinkled face "—I heard what sounded like a kitten. The closer I got, though, I realized it was a baby cooing softly."

"Emma?" Zane said, with apparently enough surprise to please Alonzo.

The man clapped his hands. "Someone had left

her beside the road wrapped in a dirty towel." He shook his head in disbelief even after all these years.

Zane was still in shock. "What did you do with her?"

"I brought her home, what else? I am no fool." He chuckled and gave his guest a wink. "I knew this little bundle of joy would keep Maria from being so upset with me."

"You raised her as your own?"

"We had always wanted children," he said with a shrug. "This one came from God. Try to explain that to Social Services. Much easier for us to let everyone think Maria had given birth at home. Maria named her Emma after a character in a book she liked. The moment I saw her red hair I told Maria we'd have to give her a name that goes with that hair."

"So that's where the McDougal came from," Zane guessed.

"Emma McDougal Alvarez. Never was there a more cheerful child or a more mischievous one," he said with obvious affection. "She grew up here, making our lives blessed. We wanted her to go to college, but then Maria died." He shook his head. "Emma didn't want to leave me here alone, so she stayed for a while until I made her leave." A sadness came into his eyes.

"Something happened to her?" Zane asked, remembering what the people she'd worked with at the hotel in Denver had said. They had sensed some tragedy in her, perhaps the death of a husband or husband and child.

"She met a man. A bad man."

RAFE GRABBED JINX and dragged her to her feet. She told herself not to fight him, but as he pulled her up, she saw his men dragging Dawson's limp body behind the cabin.

"No," she cried and fought to get away. "You killed him?"

"Who is he?" Rafe demanded, shaking her into submission. "Who is your accomplice?"

When she didn't answer, he shook her harder.

"His name is Dawson Chisholm."

Rafe swore. "This is why you wanted to hit this ranch? You've been working with him all along?"

"Don't be stupid," she said and realized at once that was the wrong thing to say to a man like Rafe.

He backhanded her across the mouth.

She wiped her bleeding lip and glared at him. "He came up here to check his cattle and caught me. I've been his prisoner ever since."

Rafe gave her a scathing look. "You really do think I'm stupid, don't you? I saw the two of you ride in here together. You thought you could double-cross me?"

Jinx felt too sick to answer. She wanted to curl up and die. They'd killed Dawson. She started to slump back to the ground, but Rafe slammed her against the stone well, holding her up by a fistful of her jacket in his beefy hand. "How many others are there?"

She shook her head. "There aren't any others." She could tell he didn't believe her. "But when his five brothers find out what you've done..."

Rafe swore and shoved her toward her horse. "You try to make a run for it and I will personally shoot you," he said as his men came around the side of the house.

What had they done with Dawson's body? Her heart ached. She'd warned herself not to fall for him. But she had. And she'd gotten him killed. If the rustlers had hit any other ranch but Chisholm Cattle Company... Jinx knew that any rancher could have caught one of them and ended up like her father and Dawson, but still it wasn't any rancher who'd gotten killed. It was Dawson.

"Let's get these calves down to the rest of the herd," Rafe ordered.

Jinx realized that the dust she'd seen on the horizon hadn't been the rustlers at all. Dawson must have seen it and thought the same thing. No wonder they both hadn't been suspicious of an ambush.

But Rafe hadn't driven the cattle any farther than just over the hill into a lush meadow. She saw the dark Angus cattle, heard the mothers begin to respond to the sounds of their bawling calves and move toward them.

Past the cattle, she saw the second abandoned

ranch house set back against a hill with some out-buildings around it.

"She's going with us?" one of the rustlers de-manded. They hadn't moved toward their horses.

Rafe laid his hand over the six-gun on his hip. "She's going with us as far as the trucks in case any more Chisholms show up. She is now our hostage."

The men looked as if they would have preferred Rafe kill her and leave her here with Chisholm, but they didn't put up an argument. Jinx knew that any one of them would gladly shoot her. They'd killed twice now. What was another body to get rid of out here in the middle of nowhere?

Jinx glanced toward the old cabin as Rafe led her horse and her toward the waiting cattle and the small ranch house. Now that he wasn't looking, she let the tears come.

I'm so sorry, Dawson. So sorry. Forgive me.

But she knew she would never forgive herself.

AGGIE BROUGHT EMMA DINNER—another sandwich, an apple and more coffee.

Emma wasn't one to complain. She poured herself a cup of coffee and took a drink, needing the warmth. She couldn't help but think of Hoyt in jail, both of them prisoners.

"I'll bring you an extra sandwich in the morning," Aggie said.

"Why?" Emma asked, instantly suspicious.

"There is something I need to do, but don't worry, I'll be back later in the day."

She put down the coffee, having suddenly lost her appetite. "Don't hurt my family."

Aggie cocked a brow at her. "*Your* family?"

"I mean it. Do whatever you want with me, but leave the boys alone."

Aggie laughed. "The boys seem to be out of control over at the house. They got into a huge fight after the sheriff stopped by to talk to them this morning."

Emma felt sick. Her stepsons needed her more than ever with their father in jail. "You have to let me go to them. What is the point of keeping me here anyway?"

"Do you have any idea what evidence the sheriff might have wanted to show them?"

She shook her head. "Don't you? You hear everything that is going on at that house. Aggie, this is crazy, surely you realize that? What is it you hope to hear over there?"

"You wouldn't believe me if I told you."

"Try me," Emma said, although she suspected Aggie was right.

"I told you. Your life is in danger and someone is trying to frame your husband for murder. I'm just trying to prove it."

Emma shook her head and laughed. "*You're* the one who is trying to frame Hoyt for even *your* murder. You're the one who drugged me and now has me locked up here."

Aggie shook her head. "I knew you wouldn't believe me any more than the sheriff would if I took my story to her. There's more going on here than you know," she said mysteriously.

Emma groaned as Aggie moved to the door.

"You're just going to have to trust that I know what I'm doing."

Good luck with that, Emma thought but wisely didn't say as the woman left, locking the door behind her.

THE THUNDERSTORM that had been brewing on the horizon moved in so quickly, it seemed to take them all by surprise. They moved the calves down to the meadow, turning them out to find their mothers. The noise from the cows and their bawling calves at first hid the sound of thunder on the horizon.

Jinx noticed the wind first. It picked up, bending the tall tops of the pines and sending dust devils whirling across the patch of dirt in front of the old ranch house.

She squinted as dust filled the air. The clouds snuffed out the last of the light as they moved in. It felt as if someone had dropped a dark blanket over them.

Jinx felt nothing. A numbness had settled into her bones. She sat on her horse knowing that the rustlers were watching her, almost daring her to take advantage of the storm to make a run for it.

She knew if she made an abrupt move, one of them would shoot her and take their chances with Rafe. She saw him ride away for a moment to talk to his men, but she knew he was watching her out of the corner of his eye.

Any other time she might have taken her chances, spurred her horse and tried to make the top of the hill behind the old ranch house. She could see the deep eroded gullies around it and a part of her knew if she could reach one of them, she would get away.

But all the fight had gone out of her. Dawson was dead. She'd gotten him killed.

Lightning splintered the dark sky, followed only moments later by a burst of thunder that boomed as if right over their heads. The first drops of rain were hard and cold and made her stir as if she'd been in a daze.

Rafe grabbed her reins again and rode her over to the house. "Take care of the horses," he yelled to one of his men as he dragged her from her mount and shoved her toward the front door.

The huge drops of rain slanted down, stinging as they struck, the wall of rain obliterating everything around them. In a flash of lightning, Rafe threw open the front door and shoved her inside the dark cold house. Thunder rumbled around them.

She heard Rafe turn the skeleton key in the lock.

Not that he probably needed to. She suspected he'd told his men not to come near the house no matter what they heard.

Jinx turned toward him, realizing what he had planned. She could barely see him in the darkness except when lightning flashed through the windows. She shivered, suddenly aware of the cold and her wet clothing that now stuck to her skin.

He let out a soft chuckle. "Now it's just you and me, Miss Brittany Bo 'Jinx' Clarke."

She felt the numbness leave her. He knew who she was. So he also knew why she was here. She thought she'd feel more fear knowing what this meant. Instead, her anger and need for justice rushed through her with a renewed fire.

"The boss really wants to see you."

"Oh yeah? I really want to see him," she said. She knew now why he hadn't killed her. He was taking her to the boss. Isn't that what she'd always wanted?

She tried not to let herself think about the cost.

"By the way, who is the boss?"

He laughed and shook his head. "Not so fast, sweetheart."

Jinx stepped to Rafe, catching him off guard as she pressed her palms to his chest. "Why don't we go meet him right now? Or did you have something else in mind?"

In a burst of lightning, she saw him grin as he

pressed his body to hers. "And here I thought I was going to have to force you."

She smiled up at him. "I've played enough poker to know when to throw in my hand."

Rafe chuckled. "I've been looking forward to this."

"Me, too." Jinx pulled his gun quickly, but Rafe surprised her with the speed with which he reacted. He grabbed for the pistol as she stepped back, his hand clamping down on her wrist.

She struggled to free herself as his other hand shot out to grab a handful of her hair.

"I was hoping you'd put up a fight," Rafe said, anger making his voice sound like sandpaper as he jerked her against him, both of them still struggling for the weapon. "You're going to regret this."

Jinx already regretted it. Her plan had been to walk him out of here at gunpoint. Force him to take her to his boss. End this once and for all.

Rafe was twisting her wrist and she could feel the weapon slipping from her fingers. Once he had the gun—

The gunshot boomed inside the empty old house like the blast of a cannon. It echoed around her, the surprise of the sound making her freeze.

Rafe released his grip on her as he grabbed his chest. In a flash of lightning, he dropped to his knees in front of her. Thunder rumbled, rattling the windows.

"He'll kill you," Rafe said through gritted teeth.

"Tell me who you're working for," she said, dropping beside him.

He looked at her dumbly. She could see pain and shock in his eyes.

"Tell me," she pleaded.

He opened his mouth. A bubble of blood appeared at the corner of his lips. As another bolt of lightning splintered the sky outside, he fell face-first onto the dirty wooden floor.

Jinx stumbled back, her heart in her throat. "No!" For a moment she was too shocked and upset to think clearly.

At a sound beyond the broken window, she spun around, realizing the men might have heard the gun blast over the storm and would be busting down the door any moment. Thunder cracked overhead. Lightning illuminated the two of them in flickering flashes, followed by another crack of thunder that seemed to shake the floor under her as she stood, trembling, the gun dangling at her side.

What was she going to do now?

Chapter Ten

Dawson came to slowly. At first all he felt was cold. Then came the pain, the confusion. He blinked for a moment, thinking he'd gone blind.

The darkness was total. He blinked again. Something sticky ran down into his eye and when he raised his hand to the spot over his eye, his fingers came away wet with blood from a gash in his forehead.

He wiped the blood away and tried to sit up, suddenly aware of his shoulder. It, too, was wet with blood. He lay there for a moment breathing in the damp, musty air. He could hear what sounded like gunfire outside and, between the volleys, could hear what sounded like rain. Under him he felt cold dirt and sensed he was underground.

With the memory of what had happened, he pushed himself up, fighting the pain; his only thought was of Jinx.

"Jinx?" he said as he felt around on the cold floor. "Jinx?" He listened but heard nothing but the haunting echo of his own voice. Reaching out in front of him, he felt something cold and solid. A rock wall. He inched his fingers along it until he came to what felt like weathered wood. A door? He discovered a hinge and pulled himself to his feet, using the wall for balance until the dizziness subsided.

The doorknob was ice-cold to the touch. He turned it. The door swung open and the space filled with a dim, rain-streaked light. He stumbled out into a small covered space that ended in a row of stairs leading upward.

He could hear the thunder now, see flashes of lightning. Breathing in the sweet scent of rain, he stepped back out into the downpour. He still felt wobbly on his feet, but some of his strength was coming back.

Glancing back, he made sure that Jinx wasn't in a corner of what he saw was an old root cellar that had been dug back under the house. His attackers had shot him and thrown him down here, probably thinking no one would find his body.

But where was Jinx?

Dawson began to climb the steps, his memory coming back to him as he mounted each old stone step. The rustlers had waited in ambush and attacked. He told himself he should have known they would do that. Hadn't they already killed one man?

But he hadn't anticipated an attack. He'd believed that they were more interested in his cattle. Apparently they were more worried about Jinx than he'd thought they would be.

Still, something niggled at the back of his mind. First her father, and now they were after Jinx. Probably had Jinx. The thought sent his heart pounding. What would they do to her? He hated to think.

With dread, he went to find her.

The thunderstorm snuffed out most of the day's light. Low clouds hung over the ranch yard. Through the driving rain he saw the spot next to the wishing well where he'd last seen Jinx.

Their horses were gone. No big surprise there. As he moved through the downpour, he looked for any sign of her and saw nothing. The old cabin was small and empty. At the wishing well, he stopped and looked down. The well was too narrow to stuff a body down. He felt relieved, though only a little.

After a quick search, it was clear.

Jinx was gone.

So were the cattle and his horse. The rustlers had taken her. As he bandaged his shoulder as best he could and washed the blood from his face, he told himself that their taking her alive was a good sign. They had left him for dead and could have done the same thing with her. He had to assume they had a reason for keeping her alive—at least for the time being.

Though he wasn't fool enough to think she was safe. If anything, he was all the more worried about her. Where would they take her? In a flash of lightning he looked down the mountain toward the prairie. They wouldn't be crazy enough to try to move the cattle in a thunderstorm, would they?

For a moment he thought he heard the mooing of his cattle. He moved toward the sound, climbing up the small hill behind the cabin. At the top he waited for another crack of lightning. He didn't have to wait long. The sky lit up, illuminating a ranch house in the distance and a large herd of black cows.

Relief washed over him like the pouring rain. He watched, trying to estimate how many of them there might be. He'd seen at least one rider and knew there would have to be several watching the herd. The cattle would be spooked with the thunder and lightning. Just about anything could start another stampede and the cattle could scatter for miles.

In the darkness that followed the lightning strike, Dawson saw what appeared to be a small fire glowing under an overhang on an outbuilding a little way from the house. There were no lights on in the house, no sign of Jinx. But there were horses in the corral, his and Jinx's included.

Dawson knew what he had to do. The bastards had tried to kill him. They'd left him for dead. Taken his horse. And his woman.

The thought of Jinx being his woman made him smile. She would never belong to any man. But a man would be damned lucky if he could talk her into sharing her life with him.

With each step, he thought about her and how to get her away from the rustlers. He had no weapon and he'd lost just enough blood that he was unsteady on his feet. But he was alive, and with his last breath he would find a way.

He smiled to himself as he realized that he wasn't going after the rustlers for justice. Or revenge. Or even his cattle. All he wanted was Jinx.

ZANE WATCHED THE PLANE bank over the Billings rimrocks and thought about what he'd learned in California.

"I have been worrying about Emma," Alonzo had said. "She usually calls every few days to see how I am doing. I haven't heard from her yet this week."

"She doesn't come to visit?" Zane asked, surprised by that, since the two seemed close.

"She knows he has people watching the house."

"You're sure her former husband is still in prison?" he'd asked Alonzo. Apparently Emma had gotten involved with an abusive criminal who'd almost killed her. He'd ended up in prison for killing another man during a liquor-store holdup. Emma had turned him in. He'd sworn that when he got out he would find her and kill her.

"I check every week. He is still inside. But he

comes up for parole next year. It's his friends I worry about," Alonzo said, looking even more worried.

"It might not be this ex-husband or his friends." Zane told him about Aggie Wells and how the sheriff in Whitehorse was planning to set a trap in the morning and his brothers were helping.

"It's good she has such wonderful stepsons," he'd said. "I don't want to believe that our Emma married another killer."

"She didn't. My father had nothing to do with the deaths of his other wives. The sheriff thinks this Aggie Wells might be behind it. Hopefully, we'll know tomorrow."

"I know Emma loves your father. All she talked about every time I spoke with her was Hoyt this and Hoyt that. I could hear the happiness in her voice. She would never have left him if she believed he was innocent."

"My father is convinced of that, as well."

Alonzo had crossed himself and said something in Spanish he didn't understand. "You must find her."

Yes, Zane thought as the plane came into its final approach. He was beginning to think his brothers were right about Emma having never left Montana— at least not of her own free will.

Zane had promised to let Alonzo know as soon as he heard something and then he'd caught the last flight home. Now as the plane came in for the landing, he couldn't wait to get back to the ranch. He still had a three-hour drive ahead of him, but he'd called Marshall and filled him in on everything he'd found out.

His brothers were at the ranch waiting for him. In the morning, the five of them would leave early to go off to work on the new fence and leave the sheriff to spring her trap.

Zane hoped to hell it worked.

JINX MOVED AROUND the dark abandoned house cautiously. She didn't dare use the flashlight she'd found on Rafe. After she'd realized that the other rustlers must not have heard the gunshot over the noise of the storm, she'd searched Rafe, finding another gun, a knife and the flashlight. She tucked the knife sheath into the top of her boot, stuffed one of the pistols into her waistband and held on to the one that had killed Rafe.

She avoided his body. She was shaking, from the cold and rain, from what had happened with Rafe.

She'd killed a man.

That realization, she knew, hadn't completely settled in yet. Right now she just had to concentrate on getting away from the other rustlers. If they found out she'd killed Rafe, she had no doubt what they would do to her.

Jinx checked the windows and saw where the other rustlers had gone. Through the pouring rain she could make out an old shed against the hillside with a lean-to on one side. They had built a fire and some of them were sitting around it. She was sure they were warmer than she was.

Counting the men around the fire, she figured three of them must be out with the cattle in the rain. She watched lightning zigzag across the open dark sky, listening as the thunder began to move off, and knew she couldn't wait much longer to make a run for it.

Even if the men were planning to spend the night here, eventually someone was going to come check on Rafe. His body lay in front of the locked door, blocking her exit. Fortunately there was a back door. In a flash of lightning she'd seen that it opened to a small gully that ran behind the house.

If she could stay down and keep moving, she might be able to get far enough from the house that the men wouldn't be able to find her.

In a burst of lightning that illuminated a corner of the house, she saw the saddlebags Rafe had brought in. She found hers and Dawson's and quickly went through them, stuffing anything she thought she might need into one and pulling on her slicker. She was still chilled and running scared.

But she knew she stood only one chance and that was to make a run for it.

Jinx moved to the door, waiting until the next lightning flash and the pitch blackness that followed it.

DAWSON SMELLED THE SMOKE and knew he had to be close. He'd been stumbling along in the darkness and pouring rain. He was soaked to the skin and chilled and couldn't tell if his light-headedness was from his loss of blood or from exhaustion and hypothermia.

He crouched down as he neared a rise and saw what was left of the old ranch buildings below him. He could see the dark cattle through the steadily falling rain and the horses penned up in the corral.

As he moved closer, staying to the gully behind the ranch house, he caught the sound of laughter, even a snatch of drunken conversation. He inched closer, anxious to see Jinx, praying she was safe.

The smell of smoke grew stronger. As he came around a bend in the gully he could see the light from the campfire under the lean-to and several of the men sitting around the fire. He listened.

If Jinx was with them, she wasn't saying anything. He had to get closer. One of the men suddenly stepped to the edge of the lean-to and looked toward the house. He said something over his shoulder to the other men.

Dawson caught only the name Rafe and the words *that woman,* followed by a raunchy laugh as the man rejoined the others.

Rafe was at the house with Jinx? Dawson felt his stomach roil at the thought. Working his way back up through the narrow gully he was almost to the back of the house when the door opened.

He stepped back and waited, hoping it was Rafe.

Jinx darted out the door only to be grabbed, spun around and slammed against the back wall of the house. Dawson pulled back his fist at the last moment. Rain pounded. Lightning lit the sky.

"Dawson!" she cried and threw herself into his arms as thunder rumbled around them. "I was so scared that you were dead." He grimaced in pain at her embrace and she quickly drew back. "How badly are you hurt?" she asked, keeping her voice down as the thunder died.

"Never mind that. Where's Rafe?" Clearly he had been expecting Rafe to come through that door—not her.

"Dead. The others are either watching the cattle or sitting by the fire under a lean-to a ways from here." She could see that he was still processing the news that Rafe was dead.

"Anyone else in the house?"

She shook her head and he reached around her to open the door, leading her back inside. Jinx hadn't wanted to go back inside. It was dark and cold in the house. Only the occasional lightning flash illuminated the space. They stood just inside the back door out of the rain.

When he glanced toward the front door and saw

Rafe's body in a flicker of lightning, she said, "It was an accident. I…" She couldn't form the words to say what Rafe had planned for her or how she'd gone for his gun—another impulsive decision that had almost cost her her life. "I didn't have a choice."

Dawson put his good arm around her and pulled her close. "Did he tell you who is behind the ring?"

She shook her head and nestled against his wet clothing, seeking the warmth beneath it. "I don't think the others will come around until morning."

"We can't take that chance," he said. "We need to get to the horses. What do you have for weapons?"

She told him, handing him his gun and Rafe's pistol, keeping her own and the knife.

"I'm going to sneak out and get us two horses," he said. "Can you get the saddles and tack?"

"Yes." She could feel his gaze on her.

"Be careful. We'll meet in the gully behind the house."

"Dawson—" She realized she'd almost blurted out that she loved him. "You be careful, too."

He disappeared out the back door, with her right behind him. The saddles and tack had been dumped on the porch of the house out of the rain. She rummaged through it quickly and as quietly as possible.

Dawson took two halters from Jinx and she watched him cross to the corral between flashes of lightning. It was far enough from the house and the lean-to that she doubted the rustlers would see him.

But if the already spooked horses started acting up, one of the rustlers might brave coming out in the rain to check.

Jinx quickly gathered up what she could carry and took it around to the back of the house out of sight of the lean-to and the men under it to wait for Dawson.

He appeared a few minutes later leading two horses. They each saddled their horses quickly. The rain was letting up, but her fingers were still red and numb by the time she finished getting her horse ready to ride.

"I want you to ride up through that gully at the back of the house and meet me on the other side of the hill," he said.

She saw that he was still in a lot of pain and his shoulder had started bleeding again. He needed medical attention. Surely he wasn't still thinking of trying to get his cattle back. "What are you going to do?"

"I'm going to open the corral and run off the horses, then you and I are headed for Chisholm Cattle Company."

"What about the cattle?" she asked.

"All I care about is getting you away from here to some place safe. If you're still determined to go after the leader of this rustling ring—"

"I just want to get you to a doctor," she said.

He leaned into her, kissed her quickly and said, "Be ready to ride, then."

JUST BEFORE DAYLIGHT, Marshall picked McCall up and brought her to the Chisholm ranch. She was hidden in the king cab seat behind him as they drove in—as per the plan. She could see the mountains in the distance and the tops of the peaks encased in clouds.

Earlier she'd thought she'd smelled rain in the air, but the forecast for the prairie was warm and dry. The sky was lightening to the east, the sun peeking out from the horizon, promising a clear, sunny day.

The other Chisholm brothers had stayed at the main house last night and had made sure that anyone listening in would know they weren't leaving until morning.

Marshall parked where he could sneak her in the back way. She had her radio and deputies planted out of sight at strategic points on the roads so they could see anyone coming in or out of the ranch. They had been advised to simply report if they saw someone and not to apprehend.

McCall hoped they weren't all wasting their time.

As she slipped into the back of the house, the Chisholms went about their business, making themselves sack lunches as she took a look around. She looked for a comfortable place to wait, since she didn't know how long it might take.

There was a good chance that Aggie Wells wouldn't show, because she was dead and buried somewhere on the ranch. It wouldn't be the first time

McCall had been wrong about a suspect. It took a kind of killer mentality to start from nothing and build an empire the way Hoyt Chisholm had. McCall reminded herself that she could be dead wrong about him and that would make Emma dead wrong, as well.

Finding a stool in the kitchen, she dragged it into the large walk-in pantry, leaving the door open a crack so she had a view of the kitchen table and the back door.

A few minutes later the brothers waved goodbye and made a show of leaving to go string barbed wire on the fence they were building too far from the house to return unexpectedly.

McCall listened as they drove away and a deathly quiet fell over the house. She thought about the way it must have sounded when all six sons and Hoyt and Emma and several hired help had been in this big old place. She also thought about the first time she'd met Emma and how much she'd liked her. It was clear just looking around the house that Emma had made it a home.

Now the place was empty. The brothers had been staying here to hold down the fort until their father was exonerated. If that happened. They were all old enough that they would soon want to go back to their own places, get on with their lives—no matter what happened with their father.

But she did wonder what would happen to Chisholm Cattle Company if Hoyt was found guilty. The brothers would try to keep the place going without him, but Hoyt had been the heart and soul of the ranch.

At the sound of a floorboard creaking, McCall started. She eased her weapon out of the holster, telling herself it was an old house. Old houses creaked and groaned. Another floorboard creaked and then another. The sound was coming from the living room. Whoever it was, was headed this way.

McCall stood and pressed her body against the pantry wall so she had a good view of the person who was about to appear in the kitchen doorway.

As JINX RODE UP through the dark gully, the rain had slowed to a drizzle, but she barely felt it she was so worried about Dawson.

Her heart suddenly leaped to her throat as she heard shouts behind her, then the boom of gunfire. She looked back, but saw nothing through the rain and darkness. It took every ounce of common sense she had not to turn around and go back. Spurring her horse, she stopped at the edge of the hill. She could see the cattle were huddled in a shimmering sea of black bodies against the first signs of daybreak. No sign of any rustlers.

Reining in, she turned and stared back into the darkness of the hillside, telling herself Dawson would come riding over the rise at any moment. She saw movement, heard more shouts and gunfire. The cattle began to mill and bawl.

Jinx blinked as a rider emerged from the rain and darkness. She held her breath. As the figure drew closer, she felt her chest swell with relief. Dawson. Tears burned her eyes. Her heart felt as if it might burst.

She glanced behind him, expecting to see rustlers coming over the hill as he rode up to her. His face was etched in pain and she feared they would never make it to the ranch. He gave her a smile, even though she could tell it cost him. The rain had almost stopped. A fine mist hung in the air, making all of it seem surreal.

As they reined their horses around and rode into the new day, she looked back at the cattle. She could smell smoke from the rustlers' fire. Hear voices. Two rustlers on foot topped the hill as she and Dawson rode into the trees.

Rifle fire punctuated the wet morning air, but the men were too far away and their shots never reached the trees.

Jinx thought about the cattle they were leaving and wondered if Dawson would ever get any of them back. Or would the rustlers, after finding Rafe dead, only care about retrieving their horses and saving their own necks?

Dawson had come for her—not his cattle.

It filled her heart like helium and yet, as she rode,

she couldn't help the feeling that she'd failed in so many ways. She'd almost gotten Dawson killed and herself as well and she still didn't know who was behind the rustling ring, who was ultimately responsible for her father's death.

She shivered in the cold as water dripped from the dark green branches of the pines and glanced over at Dawson. This wasn't over yet, she thought, realizing how weak he was. Nothing else mattered, she realized, but getting him to a doctor. She couldn't let him die. Not after everything they'd been through. She hadn't even gotten a chance to tell him that she loved him.

Chapter Eleven

Aggie Wells came into the kitchen as if she lived there. She carried a small box that she set on the table before she headed back into the living room.

McCall watched her from her hiding place in the pantry, but lost her when she left the kitchen. She could hear her in the living room and dining room. She seemed to just be wandering around the house.

McCall wondered if she was pretending she lived here. Her former supervisor had suggested that Aggie might have gotten too involved with Hoyt Chisholm and his case, that she had fallen in love with Hoyt.

The insurance company Aggie had worked for let her go after they found out she was still working the case on her own time—even after her investigation had been unable to prove anything other than Laura Chisholm's drowning had been an accident.

Aggie came back into the kitchen, shoved one of the chairs closer to the table and stood on it. Reaching into the box she'd brought, she took out what looked like a small smoke alarm and replaced the one the Chisholm brothers had destroyed.

She worked with a single-minded efficiency, making McCall wonder how many other houses she had bugged over the years.

McCall frowned as she realized she hadn't heard a vehicle. How had Aggie gotten here? Not by a road, or one of the deputies would have alerted McCall.

As Aggie finished reinstalling the listening device, she froze on the chair and looked around as if she suddenly sensed she wasn't alone. She lowered herself off the chair to the kitchen floor, clearly trying to be as quiet as possible, picked up her box and slipped out the back door.

McCall was ready to pitch the plan. Aggie had been spooked. What would she do? McCall couldn't bear to think that the woman might just take off and never be seen again. But what if she *had* taken Emma and was now going back to wherever she'd hidden her?

Arresting Aggie now might mean never finding Emma. McCall made herself stay where she was, counting to ten before she eased out of the pantry.

She caught a whiff of perfume as she edged to the back door and peered out. Aggie was a few hundred yards from the house, walking toward a four-wheeler.

McCall swore. That's why the deputies hadn't seen her. She hadn't taken a road, but had come across country.

Grabbing her radio, she barked out an order for the deputies to close in. Now! "She's on a four-wheeler." She opened the back door, heard the four-wheeler crank over and saw Aggie take off through the pasture.

McCall realized the deputies couldn't possibly get there fast enough. Aggie was going to get away unless—

She raced through the house, slowing at the front door. It was standing wide open. She got another strong whiff of perfume. Why would Aggie leave the front door open?

McCall didn't have time to consider what it might mean as she sprinted to the corral. She'd never had a horse of her own, but she'd ridden any horse that would let her since she was a girl. Because of it, riding bareback was the only way she knew how to ride.

One of the horses came toward her. She grabbed a halter off the post by the gate and, slipping it on, led the mare out of the corral and swung up onto her back. Spurring the horse, she went after Aggie as the wind whipped the cottonwoods, sending dust swirling around her. In the distance she could see storm clouds over the mountains and smell rain in the air. The weatherman had been wrong.

As she rode the horse over the first rise, she caught sight of Aggie tearing through the open country on the four-wheeler. Dust churned up behind the rig, obscuring the rider. Even if Aggie looked back, she wouldn't be able to see McCall coming after her.

McCall leaned over the mare's neck and galloped across the pasture, keeping her focus on the four-wheeler and where it was headed.

DAWSON TOPPED THE LAST RISE and saw Chisholm Cattle Company sprawled below him. He reined in his horse. He'd never seen anything more beautiful in his life. Except for the woman who rode up next to him.

She smiled over at him and he saw her concern. She must see how hard it was for him to even stay in the saddle he felt so weak.

"You going to make it?" she asked.

He smiled back at her. "I am now."

As they rode down toward the ranch, he saw dust boiling up along the road into the ranch. Two sheriff's deputy vehicles came racing up the road toward them.

Jinx rode out to flag down one of the deputies. "Dawson's been shot by some rustlers. He needs medical attention right away," she said.

As Dawson rode up, he recognized the deputy as his future sister-in-law Halley Robinson. She started to reach for her radio, no doubt to call an ambulance.

"There isn't time," Jinx said. "We need to take him in your patrol car."

Dawson felt the last of his strength seep out of

him. He slumped over his saddle, only to feel some-one pulling him down and into the patrol car. He lay back against the seat for a moment before Jinx drew him over, cradling his head in her lap. He felt her fingers brush back a lock of hair from his forehead, heard her say, "Please hurry."

The sound of the siren came on and he felt the patrol car turn around and head toward town. He closed his eyes.

"Listen to me, Chisholm," Jinx whispered next to his ear. "I didn't ride all the way off that mountain to have you die on me now." He heard the emotion in her voice and realized she was close to tears.

He opened his eyes, looked into her adorable face and tried to smile. That was the last thing he remembered.

McCall slowed the mare to a trot as she saw the four-wheeler turn onto an old dirt road. At the end of it sat an empty farmhouse. She eased the mare through the trees along the edge of a creek that ran the length of the property as she watched the four-wheeler come to a stop behind the farmhouse and Aggie climb off to disappear inside.

McCall kept to the trees, working her way to the back of the house, all the time keeping an eye on the dust-coated windows. Was Emma inside? She could only hope.

She thought about calling for backup as she slid

from her horse, but a patrol car could be spotted for miles out here and McCall couldn't chance what Aggie might do to Emma. If Emma was even in there.

No, she thought as she drew her weapon and moved stealthily toward the back door. She couldn't risk Emma's life by tipping off Aggie they were onto her, and she had a strong feeling that Emma was inside.

The back door wasn't locked. It swung open with a creak that made McCall grimace. The old, bare kitchen was empty. She stepped inside. As she moved toward the front of the house, she heard voices upstairs.

Her heart soared. Aggie wasn't alone. Someone was with her. Emma?

Weapon in hand, McCall started up the stairs. Normally she would be thinking about what she was going to find at the top of the steps, but suddenly she had a flash of memory of lying in bed with her husband—and the realization that she could already be pregnant, just as she'd joked with Luke last night.

The thought of having Luke's baby made her go soft inside. She hesitated on the stairs, surprised by this sudden well of emotion. McCall had never thought anything could keep her from doing her job.

And while she wouldn't let it now, she realized that having Luke's baby was going to change everything—especially the way she felt about risking her life.

She shook the thought away as she continued up the stairs, torn between her love for her job and her love for her husband and the thought of their child.

At the top of the stairs she stopped to listen, afraid the creaking stairs might have given her away. With relief she heard two women's voices coming from behind one of the closed doors. One of them was Emma's.

McCall inched toward the door, fearing it would be locked. Her hand closed over the knob. She took a breath, let it out and tried the knob. It turned in her hand.

On the count of three. One. Two. Three.

"I MEAN IT, DAWSON, don't you dare die on me, you hear me?" Jinx said as she cradled his head in her lap. He looked so pale and yet so handsome. Her heart broke at the sight. She checked his pulse again. He was still alive, but he'd lost so much blood....

She felt that if she kept talking to him, she wouldn't lose him. She whispered to him as the deputy drove, talking about anything she could think of, her childhood, her first boyfriend, her dreams, her hopes.

"I wish we'd met at a community dance, that you saw me from across the room and that you worked your way through the crowd, determined to dance with me," she whispered. "Our first dance would be a slow one and you would hold me close and—" her voice broke "—and you would never let me go."

She felt tears burn her eyes as the deputy said, "Once we get to the hospital, I'm going to have to get your statement about who shot him."

Jinx glanced up and nodded to the deputy looking at her in the rearview mirror, then started as she felt Dawson move in her lap, his voice a hoarse whisper.

"What's your real name?"

She looked down and saw that his eyes were open and he was staring up at her.

"Brittany Bo Clarke."

He smiled. "Easy to see why you go by Jinx." Then his eyes closed again.

She didn't know if he could hear her or if he had passed out again, but she kept talking to him. "I grew up on the Double TT Ranch. It was home even though we lived at the old homestead and my father was only the ranch manager all those years. My father worked for Hank Thompson. When he died his son, Lyndel, inherited the ranch."

Jinx couldn't help remembering her first run-in with Lyndel when they were both kids. Lyndel was only four years her senior, a son born to the older Hank and his young wife, who left him right after Lyndel was born.

Dawson groaned as if he sensed something unpleasant had happened with Lyndel and that was what had caused her to stop talking to him.

"My first boyfriend was a neighbor boy," she said quickly as she stroked Dawson's dark hair. "We used to swim together in the creek, ride horses, build forts, you know the kind of puppy love best friends have as kids." She wondered if there had been anyone like that in Dawson's life and realized how little they knew about each other. That seemed strange since they'd been through so much together and she was in love with him.

"I went off to college. My first boyfriend married a local girl. They have three children and raise horses. I always wanted to raise horses, live on a ranch, a ranch of my own...." Her voice broke again and she looked up to see that they had reached town.

Dawson groaned softly and she had to lean in to hear his words. "Why did they change their pattern at your ranch?"

She frowned, realizing he must be delirious and talking nonsense.

As the patrol car raced to the emergency room, sirens blaring, the staff came running out with a gurney. Jinx had to let go of Dawson as he was loaded onto it and wheeled into the emergency room.

She stood just inside the draped room, watching the doctor and nurses rushing around. "Is he going to be all right?" she asked, hating that she couldn't control the tears streaming down her face.

"He's lost a lot of blood, but it looks like a clean wound," the doctor said. "The bullet went right through the shoulder. This wound," he said, probing at the blood-dried injury on Dawson's forehead, "appears to be a graze, but you can never tell with a head wound. Are you next of kin?" She shook her head. "Family should be notified."

She watched them wheel Dawson down the hall, her heart in her throat. She realized the deputy was still waiting as well and wondered now why two sheriff's deputy patrol cars had been racing into the ranch this morning.

"What was going on at the ranch as we were riding in?" she asked the female deputy.

"I'm not at liberty to say. I am going to need your statement, though," Deputy Robinson said. She pulled out a notebook and pen.

"The doctor said I should notify his family."

"I already did. I'm engaged to Dawson's brother Colton."

Jinx nodded as she recalled that one of the brothers had gotten engaged to a sheriff's deputy.

"Why don't we start with your name?"

"Brittany Bo Clarke."

"Can you tell me what happened?"

"He was shot by rustlers," Jinx said. "Could you check with the doctor and ask how he is? *Please.* I'm so worried about him."

"You're the one who brought him out of the mountains?"

"Yes. I was afraid he wasn't going to make it. When I saw your patrol car…"

"How was it you were up there?"

Jinx had known that question was coming. She turned to look down the hallway. "Please. The doctor might tell you how he is. I have to know."

The deputy gave her a sympathetic nod, got up and, pocketing her notebook and pen, went to check on Dawson.

Jinx stood watching her go, thinking that she already had Rafe's blood on her hands. Not that she could do anything for Dawson now anyway. He was in God's hands—and the doctor's.

Suddenly Rafe's last words seemed to echo in her ears.

I see why he called you Jinx.

Her heart began to pound harder. She saw the deputy talking to a nurse, then heard the nurse say Dawson had regained consciousness, his wounds didn't appear to be life-threatening and that they were getting fluids into him and he should be fine. Dawson's words came to her. *Why did they change their pattern at your ranch?* Yes, why had they?

She said a silent prayer for Dawson, then made sure no one was looking and slipped out the back of the hospital. Once outside, she took a deep breath and ran.

MCCALL TURNED THE KNOB and eased open the door
to the upstairs room in the old farmhouse. Aggie's
back came into view, then the corner of an old mattress lying on the floor and finally Emma.

She appeared to be fine, though McCall couldn't
tell if Aggie was holding a gun on her or not.

Easing the door open a little more— The hinges
creaked and Aggie started to turn. McCall raised
the gun as the former insurance investigator swung
around in surprise.

"Don't move!" McCall ordered, relieved to see
that Aggie was unarmed except for the pistol sticking
out of her waistband. She quickly took the pistol and
forced Aggie deeper into the room. "Emma? Are you
all right?"

"Glad to see you," Emma said.

Aggie stood looking defeated. "Agatha Wells,
you are under arrest," McCall said as she cuffed the
woman and read her her rights.

"I only took Emma to protect her," Aggie said.
"You don't understand. Her life is in danger."

McCall said nothing as she radioed for backup.
"It's the old Harrington place. We'll be waiting
outside for you." She helped Emma to her feet and
led the two of them outside. She'd expected to see
Deputy Robinson first, since she'd been the clos-
est, and she was suddenly worried something had
happened. She tried to radio Deputy Robinson and
couldn't get through. Her concern grew.

What if Aggie hadn't been working alone?

"Where's Deputy Robinson?" McCall said when one of three deputies came racing up in a patrol SUV. She was anxious to get Emma back home and Aggie behind bars. A second patrol car roared up the road in a cloud of dust.

"Deputy Robinson was called away on an emergency," the deputy said so the others couldn't hear. "There's been a shooting. No details yet."

"Emma, you have to listen to me," Aggie was saying. "I know you all think I'm crazy, but the only reason I took you was to—"

McCall reminded Aggie that anything she said could be used against her as the deputy loaded Aggie into the back of the first patrol car. She asked the second deputy to please take Emma home and stay with her until one of her stepsons returned.

"Thank you," Emma said, giving the sheriff a hug before climbing into the patrol car.

"And if you wouldn't mind," McCall said, "return this horse to the Chisholm corral." She handed the deputy the reins once he was behind the wheel.

Climbing into the patrol car with Aggie Wells locked in the back, she told the deputy to take them to Whitehorse and the county jail.

"You're making a terrible mistake," Aggie said from behind the wire divider. "You're going to get Emma killed. If you'd given me just a little longer, I could have proved... Never mind. You wouldn't believe me." She fell silent, slumped in the backseat as the patrol car headed for Whitehorse.

"WHERE'S JINX?" They were the first words out of Dawson's mouth when he opened his eyes again.

"Jinx?" Deputy Robinson asked from the chair next to his bed. She appeared to have been waiting there for him to wake up.

"The woman I was with," he told his brother's fiancée, then registered her expression. "What did she do?"

"She asked me to check on you and when I turned around…"

He nodded. "She was gone. That's Jinx." He closed his eyes, hiding his disappointment. He'd hoped she would be sitting beside his bed. He should have known she would go after the leader of the ring on her own. She had before and nothing had really changed.

That wasn't true, he realized. At least not for him. He'd thought not for Jinx either.

"I need to ask you some questions," Halley said. "That is, if you're up to it. The sheriff should be here soon."

Dawson opened his eyes again. His shoulder was bandaged, and so was the spot on his forehead where a bullet had grazed him. There was an IV hooked to his arm.

The last thing he wanted to do was talk about what

had happened up on the mountain. He was sure Jinx had felt the same way. He thought about her talking all the way from the ranch to the hospital. He'd been in and out of consciousness, but he could remember most of what she'd said.

"Dawson?" Halley asked.

"Sorry, I'm not sure what I can tell you." He touched the bandage on his forehead, stalling.

"The doctor said the bullet creased your forehead, but warned that there might be some memory loss."

He wished that were the case. He could remember everything—the way it had felt to lie naked with Jinx in the tall summer grass, the sound of her laugh, the feel of her touch. He closed his eyes again at the memory, reminding himself she was gone.

"Maybe it would be better later, Halley," he said without opening his eyes. The rustlers would be long gone by now, except for Rafe, even if the sheriff could get together a posse to ride up there.

He heard Halley rise from her chair.

"Do you have any idea where we can find Jinx?" she asked.

"No." He realized the moment he heard her leave his room that he was wrong. He did know where to find Jinx.

He remembered in the patrol car on the way to the hospital when she'd stopped talking. She'd been talking about the Double TT where she'd grown up, where her father had been ranch manger, where he'd died. She'd been talking about Lyndel Thompson, the new ranch owner.

"What are you doing?" the doctor demanded as he came into the room after the deputy had left, to find Dawson disconnecting the IV from his arm.

Dr. Brian "Buck" Carrey wore a cowboy hat over his long gray ponytail. His face was tanned and weathered with deep lines around his bright blue eyes. "You're still too weak to be going anywhere, son."

"You patched me up fine, Doc." Dawson swung his legs off the gurney and stood. He felt a little light-headed, but not bad. "Where are my clothes?"

"Your family is on the way to the hospital," the doctor said, shoving back his cowboy hat. His look said he'd dealt with his share of stubborn cowboys in his day. "Anything you'd like me to tell them when they get here—other than the fact that you're a damned fool to be taking off right now?"

"Tell them our summer range cattle need to be rounded up. Oh, and have them give this to the sheriff." He scribbled a note on the pad by the bed and handed it to the doctor.

Buck sighed. "And as your personal secretary, what would you like me to say when they ask where the hell you've gone?"

"The Double TT Ranch in Wyoming. Just tell them I've gone after a woman. They'll understand."

EMMA WAS WAITING on the front porch when Marshall brought Hoyt home. She told herself she wasn't going to cry, but of course she did.

He stepped from the pickup and she ran to him, throwing herself into his arms. The sheriff had called earlier, saying Hoyt had made bail after the county attorney had heard about Aggie Wells's arrest. Hoyt's call to the governor hadn't hurt either.

"Emma," he said as he hugged her so tightly she couldn't breathe. Then he held her at arm's length and looked her over. "Are you all right?"

She nodded, unable to speak around the lump in her throat.

"God, I've missed you," he said and pulled her to him again. "I was so worried."

"But you knew I would never leave you."

He drew back to smile at her. "I knew no one could run you off, so something had to have happened."

"Aggie happened. She's crazy, Hoyt."

He nodded. "I guess when she couldn't prove I had something to do with Laura's death, she tried to frame me by killing Tasha and Krystal." He shook his head as if he couldn't believe it himself. "I'm just so glad she didn't hurt *you*."

"She seemed to really believe that she was saving me from harm by abducting me. I feel sorry for her. That perfume she was wearing—"

He glanced away for a moment. "I should have

told you right away. I recognized it. It was Laura's favorite."

Emma felt a cold chill snake up her spine. "Aggie said when she investigated a case, she tried to become the victim to understand what had happened to her. But wearing her perfume?" She shuddered as she realized just how sick Aggie really was and how lucky she was to be free from the woman.

"I'm sorry I didn't believe you when you said you smelled the perfume that day," Hoyt said.

Emma nodded, barely registering what he said. She was thinking about Aggie. "I wonder if she didn't want to become Laura? That is what must have happened. In her mind, she became Laura and couldn't bear to see you married to anyone else."

"Well, the sheriff told me they are planning to send her up to the state mental hospital in Warm Springs for a psychiatric evaluation. I'm not too sure she will ever stand trial."

"What does your lawyer say?" Emma asked, still worried.

"He thinks with Aggie's arrest I will be exonerated."

Emma let out a relieved sigh. "Oh, Hoyt, then it's finally over."

He smiled down at her, then swung her up into his arms and carried her into the house.

"Don't mind me," Marshall called after them,

a laugh in his voice. "I'll just be going now," he said as the front door closed behind his father and stepmother.

LYNDEL THOMPSON LOOKED UP as Jinx walked into the main ranch house at the Double TT without knocking. He was standing behind the large breakfast bar in the kitchen about to pour himself a cup of coffee.

Surprise registered in his expression. He let out a soft chuckle as he finished pouring his coffee and put the pot back. "Didn't expect to see you."

"Why is that, Lyndel?" She'd had a lot of time between retrieving her pickup where she'd left it on the edge of Whitehorse and the long drive to Wyoming to think. The pieces seemed to be falling into place and she wondered why it had taken her so long to figure it out.

Dawson was the one who'd made her realize she hadn't been thinking clearly since her father's murder. All the other rustling jobs had been about the cattle. Her father's had been different for a reason.

Why had the rustlers changed their pattern?

"I thought you had moved on since the funeral," Lyndel said. "Didn't think you'd have any reason to come back here."

She smiled at that as she took in the ostentatious living room. Lyndel had built the house when he'd inherited the ranch. His father had cut off supporting him years ago but on his deathbed had relented and left the ranch to his only child—except it came with a small string attached.

He'd set up the inheritance where everything had to be run through Jinx's father, a man he trusted after all these years. The only way Lyndel would have full control was when he reached forty—or when her father died. Apparently Lyndel couldn't wait the eight years.

Her father had told her that Lyndel had been spending money as if there was no tomorrow—no doubt more money than the ranch had been taking in. And now he had the ranch up for sale. Her father had been fighting him—and losing. Under a clause in the inheritance, Lyndel could have lost the ranch if her father had taken legal action.

Her father had always been a fair and understanding man. He hadn't wanted to take legal action unless necessary, thinking Lyndel would come to his senses and settle down. If her father had, though, the ranch would have gone into state conservation land and Lyndel would lose everything.

"I didn't see any cattle on the way in to the ranch," she said as she ran a finger along the expensive marble countertop.

"After the rustlers hit us, I decided maybe it was time to just lease the land and get out of the cattle business."

"That right? Well, you never did have any interest in the day-to-day running of a ranch."

His smile never reached his eyes. "Jinx, I have a feeling this isn't a social call. Why don't you just spit it out?"

"I've been doing some thinking."

He chuckled and leaned against the breakfast bar. "You sure that's a good idea, High Jinks?"

"High Jinks?"

"That's what my old man used to call you. Somewhere along the way it got shortened to Jinx."

She hadn't known where she'd gotten the nickname, just that everyone had called her Jinx as far back as she could remember. But, she reminded herself, Rafe had known where she'd gotten the name.

"What's on your mind?" Lyndel asked impatiently.

She studied him, remembering the mean, selfish boy he'd been and how he used to rub it in her face that she was just the ranch manager's kid while his daddy owned the ranch. He used to brag that someday it would be his and he could kick her and her daddy off it if he wanted to.

Well, now it was his and he was selling the ranch that had meant so much to his father—and to her own.

"I know how angry you were when you found out the ranch came with strings," she said.

"Is there a point to this?" Lyndel asked, putting

down his coffee cup. He hadn't offered her a cup, but then that was no surprise.

"I met a friend of yours recently," she said. "Rafe Tillman."

He frowned and shook his head. "Doesn't ring a bell."

"Think harder. He knows *you*. That is, he *knew* you. He's dead."

Lyndel lifted a brow. "If I'd known him, maybe that would mean something to me. But—"

"That's funny, since he knew about my nickname."

"Maybe he knew my father." His voice had taken on an irritated clipped tone.

She slipped out of her jean jacket and casually hung it over the back of one of the breakfast bar's chairs. "He had something interesting to say before he died."

She had Lyndel's attention now. "You were with him?"

"Oh, didn't I mention? I hooked up with the rustlers."

"Why would you do—" The rest of his words seemed to catch in his throat. So he hadn't known that Rafe had let her join the gang. That shouldn't have surprised her. Rafe wasn't completely stupid. Lyndel wouldn't want him adding another rustler without his permission—let alone a woman. Any fool would know how much trouble that could cause among the gang of men.

But if Lyndel hadn't known, then that meant none of the other rustlers had told him. Because they hadn't known who was behind the rustling ring.

"They killed my father," she reminded him.

"So why would you have anything to do with them?"

"To get to the ringleader. I knew eventually Rafe would tell me who was behind it."

Lyndel had gone stone still.

"You killed my father."

"What are you talking about?" He picked up his coffee cup again and took a sip, avoiding her gaze. "Too bad this Rafe character is dead, because without him to verify your story…"

She shook her head. "I was so upset about what happened I wasn't thinking straight at first, but as someone pointed out to me, everything about the rustling on the Double TT didn't fit the rustlers' normal pattern."

"You're talking foolishness. If you had a shred of proof you wouldn't be standing here, you'd be talking to the sheriff." He was back to his usual cocky self as he came around the end of the breakfast bar. "Now, get the hell out of my house."

"Why? Why did you have to kill him?"

He shook his head. "If you don't leave right now—"

"What are you going to do? Call the sheriff? Maybe you should. Maybe he would like to look at the ranch books. My father must have realized that you were up to something. Is that why you had to get rid of him?"

Lyndel smiled again, the old meanness coming back into his eyes as he advanced on her. "If the sheriff was to take a look at the ranch books he would find that your father had been stealing from the ranch for years."

"That's a bald-faced lie!"

He laughed. "Hard to prove otherwise, now, isn't it?"

"That's why you had him killed. He knew what you'd been doing. I remember him saying that your father wasn't fool enough to leave you the ranch without some kind of protection against you either running it into the ground or selling your legacy. The only way you could have the ranch to do as you pleased was to kill my father."

Lyndel swore under his breath. "If you want to blame someone, blame my old man. He gave me no choice."

"You would have gotten the ranch free and clear once you were forty."

"Forty?" He snorted. "It was *my* legacy, not your father's. I had every right to do whatever I wanted with this place. I was sick to death of hearing how I couldn't spend my own money. I should have killed him the moment I inherited the place, then I wouldn't have had to listen to his lectures."

Jinx let out a gasp. She'd known, and yet hearing Lyndel say it was like a stab through the heart.

"And you should have left things alone," he snapped.

As he took another step toward her, she pulled the gun.

He froze. His gaze went from the gun to her face. His smile returned. "You can't pull the trigger."

She ran her finger lightly over the trigger. "Try me."

He'd killed her father in cold blood and for what? Money, power, freedom from anyone telling him what to do? She had told herself that when she found the man behind the rustling ring, she would kill him. One shot through the heart—just like her father's death had felt to her.

But she could still hear the boom of the gunshot that had killed Rafe. She could still remember the feel of his warm blood on her hands and the way he had looked at her before he died.

She swung the gun to the right and touched off a shot. A large pottery vase exploded, sending shards spraying across the living room as the sound of the shot echoed through the house. She quickly swung the gun back to point at Lyndel's heart.

"Are you crazy?" he demanded. "I should have told them to wait to kill your father when you were home visiting him so you would be gone, too. My mistake."

Her finger skimmed over the trigger of the gun. Just a little pressure and—

Strong arms looped around her. The gun was wrenched painfully from her hand. She struggled, but it was useless in this bear of a man's arms.

"What kept you, Slim?" Lyndel demanded. "I buzzed the barn ten minutes ago."

Chapter Twelve

Dawson drove south down into the Missouri Breaks, across the dark green river, headed for Wyoming. The drive was long, especially with him worrying about Jinx the whole time. He'd tried calling the Double TT but the line had been disconnected and Lyndel Thompson had an unlisted number.

Why would the ranch line be disconnected? He tried not to panic, but in his gut he knew something was terribly wrong.

He'd had a lot of time to think about what had happened up in the mountains, a lot of time to think about Jinx.

Brittany Bo Clarke. He smiled, thinking how the tomboy he'd bet she'd been would have wanted to be rid of a name like that. No frilly dresses and pretty pink bows, not for that little girl.

He recalled that she'd told him her mother had died when she was young and the aunt who had helped raise her had instilled the need for Jinx to be her own woman. The lessons she'd learned on the ranch with her father and her aunt had certainly done that.

Ahead he could see the outline of a huge house on the horizon. He slowed. There was a new Cadillac parked out front and an older model pickup. Both had Wyoming plates.

He wondered if the pickup belonged to Jinx. He hadn't asked her how she'd gotten to Montana and he wondered now how she'd made it back to Wyoming unless she'd had a vehicle.

As he parked and climbed out of the ranch truck he'd gotten Marshall to bring him at the hospital, he knew it wasn't like Jinx to leave her horse back in Montana. Whatever had sent her hightailing it down here must have been damned important. No way had she run to avoid the law. No, she had something else on her mind and he knew what it was.

The door was gigantic. He rang the bell and waited, feeling his anxiety growing with each passing moment. The ranch was for sale, so why had the main phone line been disconnected? Or was that the reason? Maybe it had already sold.

Dawson thought about Jinx's father. He'd been ranch manager. Had he known that Lyndel was selling the ranch? Or did Lyndel make that decision after his ranch manager was killed by the rustlers?

A large burly man opened the door. From the looks of him, he was one of the hired hands. Or Lyndel's muscle.

"I'm looking for Jinx."

"You have the wrong house," the man said in a gravelly voice. He started to close the door.

Dawson stuck his boot in it. "Then I'd like to see Lyndel Thompson."

The ranch hand scowled, a warning look in his gaze. Muscle, Dawson thought, but he was ready to go through this man if that was what it was going to take—even injured.

"Mr. Thompson isn't—"

"I know he's home, unless that's your Caddy out front, which I'm betting not," Dawson interrupted. "Tell him Dawson Chisholm is here to see him and I'm not leaving until I do."

The ranch hand started to make a threatening move when Lyndel Thompson stepped into view and said, "That's all right, Slim, I'll take care of this."

Dawson had met Hank Thompson on several occasions over the years when he'd attended cattleman meetings for the regional northwest. Lyndel was tall like his father, but that was about the only trait he seemed to have gotten from him. There was a softness to the younger Thompson, a weakness about the mouth and chin and definitely a lack of kindness in the eyes.

While Hank Thompson had been a working rancher, his son was a drugstore cowboy who Dawson would bet had never had manure on his boots. He was decked out in a fancy Western shirt, expensive jeans and boots and a brand-new Stetson as if he'd just come into some money.

"Mr. Chisholm," Lyndel said, sounding amused to find him standing at his door. Dawson was a little surprised that Lyndel knew who he was and it made him all the more convinced that Jinx was here and Lyndel had been expecting him. "What brings you all the way down from Montana? I heard there was trouble at your ranch. Seems you were in the middle of it," Lyndel said, motioning to the bandage on Dawson's forehead.

"I want to see Jinx."

He raised an eyebrow. "What makes you think she's here?" Slim was standing just a few feet away, his big arms crossed over his expansive chest, waiting as if expecting trouble.

Dawson thought about the Chisholm ranch. His father, while wealthy by most people's standards, had never had the need for a bodyguard. Why did Lyndel?

"I know Jinx came to see you," Dawson said as he pushed past the man into the opulent living room.

"Do you want me to throw him out?" Slim asked, hustling after him.

The main house at the Chisholm ranch was elegant but nothing like this. Lyndel had gone all out. Dawson said as much.

"Thank you," Lyndel said, not realizing it hadn't necessarily been a compliment. He motioned to Slim to back off. Slim pulled up his jeans and puffed out his chest to look as menacing as possible but stayed where he was. Until that moment, Dawson hadn't noticed the pistol the man had strapped to his leg.

"Don't you mean Brittany Bo Clarke?" Lyndel smiled. "I'm sorry, you just missed her."

Dawson returned his smile. "Mind telling me what she wanted with you?"

"As a matter of fact, I do. It's personal. You may not be aware of this, but Brittany Bo and I go way back from the time we were kids here on the ranch."

"Then you probably know how she got the nickname."

Lyndel chuckled. "My father gave it to her. It was actually High Jinks because of all the trouble she got into around the ranch. She really was quite the rascal, that girl." He smiled as if remembering her fondly.

"You also must know then how badly she wants the person behind the rustling ring who is responsible for her father's death."

"Yes, a horrible accident," Lyndel said.

"She seems to think it wasn't an accident. That someone wanted him dead and gave the rustlers the order to kill him."

Lyndel shook his head. "That sounds like our Jinx. She was always imaginative. Why would anyone want to kill my ranch manager?"

"I was hoping you might have some idea," Dawson said as he took a look around the living room. It opened into the kitchen. "I'm sure that's why Jinx came to see you." A wide, long hallway apparently led to the bedrooms, since the house was all on one sprawling level.

"She came to see me partly because of the good news, if you must know," Lyndel said. "The local sheriff called me earlier to tell me that the leader of the rustling ring was found dead up in Montana on your ranch. He was found shot to death after a botched attempt to rustle your cattle. I doubt I'm telling you anything you don't already know. I'm sorry, I didn't catch his name."

Had Jinx told him about riding with the rustlers and running into one of the Chisholms up in the high country? Or did Lyndel have other sources?

"You're mistaken. Rafe Tillman wasn't the leader. He had nothing to gain by killing Jinx's father," Dawson said as he stepped toward Lyndel. Slim moved in their direction, but Lyndel waved him off.

"Too bad we can't ask Rafe, isn't it?" Lyndel said as he stepped away, moving to the bar to pour himself a drink. "I'd offer you a drink, but I have an important appointment I need to get to. You can probably catch Jinx if you hurry. I would imagine she's headed into town to one of the motels. Either that or headed out of town. I understand the local sheriff is anxious to talk to her."

"As close as you say the two of you are, I'm surprised you didn't ask her to stay here," Dawson said.

"The place looks like it might be large enough for a guest or two."

Lyndel downed his drink and put down his glass a little too hard on the bar. "Now, it wouldn't be smart of me to harbor a fugitive, even one I consider a friend."

"You're so law-abiding," Dawson said sarcastically.

"I'm going to have to ask you to leave," Lyndel said, no longer pretending to be cordial.

Dawson saw that he wasn't going to get anywhere with Lyndel, and Slim was just itching to prove how tough he was. He moved toward the open front door, Slim shadowing him. "I see that your ranch is for sale."

"Not that it is any of your business, but it has already sold. I need a change of pace. I've picked up a little place in the Caribbean. Who needs the winters up here?"

Lyndel had managed to get rid of his ranch manager and his cattle to rustlers for both a profit and probably a good insurance settlement. Now he'd sold his ranch and was skipping the country. Things seem to be working out perfectly, he thought, and said as much.

"Good luck finding Jinx," Lyndel snapped from behind him.

Slim slammed the door behind him and, for a moment, Dawson stood on the front step trying to still his pounding heart.

He had spotted Jinx's battered straw hat hanging on a hook in the hallway off the living room. He'd recognized the distinctive horsehair hatband. Next to the hat had been a jean jacket that he would swear was Jinx's.

He'd also seen scuff marks on the polished floor where there had been a recent scuffle. Of course Jinx would have put up a fight.

But where was she now?

Somewhere in the house, Dawson was betting as he walked to his pickup, climbed in and drove just far enough away that Lyndel wouldn't send Slim after him.

He found a place in a creek bottom to hide the truck, then, taking his shotgun, he headed to the house on foot. He just hoped Jinx didn't do anything crazier than she already had before he could get to her.

JINX SQUIRMED. She hated cramped, confined places. That was one reason she liked the wide open spaces of Wyoming. She thought of Chisholm's Montana. The rolling prairie, the Little Rockies. She thought of the man she'd fallen in love with.

He would think she'd abandoned him, taken off to save her own neck. He would think she'd been impulsive, going off half-cocked without a plan.

She squirmed again, trying to get her hands untied. Slim had done a bang-up job binding them behind her. Her wrists ached and she couldn't feel the tips of her fingers. He'd slapped a piece of duct tape over her mouth and shoved her into some broom closet at the back of the house.

Did he really think she was going to start screaming? She knew how far the house was from anything. Who would hear her?

Unless someone had come to the house that he worried might hear her?

That was a comforting thought, but this far at the back of the house she really doubted anyone could hear her.

Only a little light bled through around the door. She'd tried throwing herself against it, but the lock had held. All she'd managed to do was hurt her shoulder. As she felt around to see if there was anything she could use to get out, she thought again of Dawson and wished she hadn't. It made her heart ache and took her mind off the problem at hand—getting out of here before Lyndel and his thug returned.

Jinx knew that Lyndel would feel he had to get rid of her. As far as he knew, she didn't have any proof he was behind the rustling ring. True, he'd admitted that he'd killed her father. But even though he could argue that it would be her word against his, she doubted he wanted to take the chance. He appeared set on selling out and getting out of Dodge.

Dawson had been right. There was a reason the rustlers had changed their pattern on the Double TT.

But his being right gave her little satisfaction. Lyndel was going to get away with murder and a lot more if she didn't get out of there.

She found some kind of cleaner on a shelf at the back, sprayed it on the rope she was bound with and tried sliding her hands out, without any luck. Feeling the clock ticking, she discovered a broom in the back corner of the closet. Using it like a lever, she pried it between the doorjamb and the knob. It took all her weight.

Just when she thought the broom handle was going to break and the splinter would probably fly off and kill her, the knob snapped off and she tumbled to the floor.

For a moment she just lay there. She'd smacked her head when she fell and hit her elbow and she'd made one devil of a racket doing it. She listened, didn't hear anything and got to her feet.

A shaft of light spilled out of the hole where the doorknob had been. Turning her back to the door, she reached her fingers inside it and jiggled the piece of metal, at the same time pushing on the door. It swung open and she stumbled out into the hallway, wondering what she was going to do now, since her wrists were still bound.

DAWSON SLIPPED ALONG the back edge of the house, keeping to the dark shadows. He'd checked the barn first and had been surprised to find a black pickup parked inside it. He'd thought the old pickup out front was Jinx's, but it must belong to one of the ranch hands. A quick check in the glove box verified it. It was Jinx's. The registration read Brittany Bo Clarke.

The keys were in the ignition and her purse was on the seat. He checked the bag, not surprised to find the gun missing that Jinx had had on her when they'd come out of the mountains.

He'd done a quick search of the barn, but no Jinx. He'd hoped that meant she was still somewhere in the house. He hadn't heard a sound coming from the house, but he'd managed to distract Slim for a while by opening a couple of the corral gates and shooing the horses toward the front of the house.

A few minutes ago he'd heard the big ranch hand swearing, then Slim and Lyndel arguing. As he neared the windows, he was glad to see one partially open. Hoping there wasn't a security alarm on the window, Dawson popped off the screen and shoved the window up enough to step inside. He didn't hear a sound, but that didn't mean that there wasn't a silent alarm.

Moving quickly through what appeared to be a guest bedroom, he opened the door to the hall and peered out. No sign of anyone. He knew Jinx was here somewhere, but he had no idea how to find her.

As he hurried as quietly as possible down the carpeted hall, he checked each room as he went. He had to assume that Slim or Lyndel had taken the

gun from Jinx. He couldn't wait to see her and ask
her what the hell she'd been thinking coming here
alone—and, worse, armed.

He opened the last door at the end of the hallway,
afraid now that he'd been wrong about Jinx being in
the house. The room beyond the doorway was huge.
So was the massive bed against one wall. He realized
he'd found the master suite, Lyndel's lair.

Dawson was about to ease the door closed again
when he heard a sound coming from what he guessed
was the master bath. He listened for a moment. Was
it possible Lyndel had hurried down here after his
argument with Slim about the horses?

Doubtful. But possible.

He shifted the shotgun to his other hand and eased
inside the room, closing the door behind him. The
sound in the bathroom stopped. He didn't move a
hair as he waited. The sound resumed and he tried
for the life of him to figure out what it was. Cautiously he stepped toward the open doorway to the
bathroom.

With shotgun ready, he peered in.

Jinx had a pair of scissors and was sawing at the
ropes that bound her wrists behind her back. She
spun around as if sensing someone behind her.

"Dawson?" She dropped the scissors and threw
herself at him.

"I know what you're thinking, Chisholm," Jinx

said as Dawson put down the shotgun and, taking the scissors, cut the rope binding her.

"You don't know what I'm thinking."

"Sure I do," she said as she tried to work some feeling back into her hands. "You're thinking, 'Jinx must have been out of her mind to come here by herself.' It isn't like I came here unarmed."

She'd noticed the relieved expression on his face when he'd seen her. He'd been unable to hold back the smile she'd caught in the bathroom mirror as he'd cut her wrists free. He hadn't been surprised that she'd gotten away—at least partially. And he'd come all the way to Wyoming for her. That had to mean something, even if he did think she was a fool.

He still didn't say anything as he put the scissors aside and picked up his shotgun again.

"Aren't you going to say anything?" she asked.

"Now that you mention it, I was going to say I think we should get out of here."

She shook her head. "Not yet. There's something I need."

He gave her a look that said he didn't believe this.

"My jean jacket. It wasn't with me in the broom closet where they left me. I need it."

"I'll buy you another jean jacket. Hell, I'll buy you two."

"Like I said, I know you think I was a fool for coming here like I did, but there's a reason I need my jean jacket. The digital recorder I bought is in it. It will have Lyndel's confession on it. He had my father killed." Her voice broke. "He admitted it."

"I'm sorry, Jinx."

She nodded. "I wanted to shoot him. I really did."

"I'm glad you didn't. As a matter of fact, I'd like to get out of here without anymore bloodshed."

"That might not be so easy."

"Lyndel said he had an appointment he was anxious to get to."

She smiled at that. "I should mention Lyndel Thompson isn't just a killer. He's a liar."

Dawson shook his head as if she amused him, the hint of a smile on his lips, and then he kissed her. She melted against him—until she heard a sound from the hallway.

Chapter Thirteen

"I told you Aggie had been in our house," Emma said to Sheriff McCall Crawford when she stopped by the ranch that evening. "Isn't that right, Hoyt?"

The three of them were sitting at the kitchen table over a cup of coffee and some warm banana bread.

"Yes, you did," McCall said. "I should have listened to you. I'm just glad you sent me that letter about the listening devices."

Hoyt smiled over at his wife. "Emma is something, isn't she?"

The sheriff smiled. "Yes, she is."

"That first time in the house, Aggie took Hoyt's bolo tie clasp and put it in Krystal's grave to frame him, just as she left her car nearby so you'd find Krystal's remains and think Hoyt had done something to her, as well," Emma said in one breath.

"That is the theory," McCall admitted.

"Surely the county attorney hasn't changed his mind about taking Hoyt to trial," Emma said, suddenly worried.

"No. The charges have been dropped."

"Unless new evidence turns up," Hoyt said, sounding skeptical that this could be over.

Emma shook her head. "Stop thinking like that, Hoyt Chisholm. It's over." She turned to the sheriff. "How is Aggie?"

"I'm surprised you'd ask, given what she's put you through," McCall said.

"I can't help it—I liked her. She was misguided, I'll admit."

"I'm afraid she might be more than that," the sheriff said. "Based on some of the statements she's made, the county attorney has decided that a psychiatric evaluation is needed. We are going to be sending her to the state mental hospital soon for testing."

Emma nodded. "I suppose she told you that she tried to become Laura Chisholm to get inside her head to find out what had happened to her, including acting like her, wearing the kind of clothes she wore and even wearing the same perfume."

McCall nodded. "She swears that she was only in your house twice. That the other time it was…" the sheriff glanced toward Hoyt before saying "…your first wife, Laura. She swears that Laura didn't drown and that she is responsible for the deaths of your second wife and third wife and that she will be coming for Emma."

Hoyt had gone white as a sheet.

Emma felt her heart jump at his reaction. He

seemed too frightened by the ramblings of a deranged woman. "You don't really believe—"

But it was the sheriff who answered. "No, I don't, but Aggie seems to. She said that was what she was trying to prove when she put the listening devices in your house."

"How does she explain knowing where Krystal's body was buried?" Emma asked.

"According to Aggie, she got a message from you to meet at that spot on the river where her car was found. It was dark when she arrived. She said she was sitting in the rental car waiting when someone attacked her and tried to kill her. She didn't see her attacker. At first she said she thought it was Hoyt. She managed to escape."

"Escape? But her car—"

"She left it because she doubted she would be believed. She said she thought that once her car was found, I would start looking into the case again. Her injuries were minor, a nosebleed, which explains the blood on the car seat. She swears she didn't know anything about Krystal's body being buried beside the river near there and only realized who her attacker had been after you, Emma, had said something about smelling her perfume three times when Aggie swears she was only in your house twice."

"That all sounds...unbelievable," Emma said. "First she blames Hoyt, then a woman who drowned more than thirty years ago?"

McCall nodded.

Hoyt still looked as if he'd seen a ghost. Emma felt her stomach knot.

"That is apparently when she put in the listening devices, hoping to catch Laura in your house," the sheriff finished. "She'd wanted ones that also supplied video, but couldn't find any that small."

"Hoyt took them all down," Emma said, getting to her feet. "We kept them as you requested in case you ever need them for evidence. But I can tell you now, I won't press charges against Aggie."

That seemed to bring Hoyt out of his shocked state. "Emma—"

"No, I liked her. Clearly she's sick. But prison isn't the place for her. She needs help."

McCall nodded and got to her feet. "Thank you for the coffee and banana bread, but I need to get going. By the way, did you get your cattle all rounded up?"

"Most of them," Hoyt said. "My sons brought the majority down earlier. They're going back up tomorrow for the ones they missed. Here, let me carry that box for you. I'll walk you out."

Emma knew her husband wanted to talk to the sheriff alone. That's why she waited, then snuck around the house to a dark corner so she could listen.

"Aggie's story about Laura, it's crazy," Hoyt said.

"Yes," the sheriff agreed as she took the box of listening devices and set them in the back of the patrol

SUV. "So why are you still worried about Emma?" she asked as she closed the car door.

"You're sure Aggie worked alone?"

"From what we can tell. There isn't any chance Laura is alive, is there?"

Hoyt rubbed a large hand over his neck as he always did when he was worried. "I can't imagine how, and yet..."

"And yet?"

"Her body was never found."

McCall nodded. "It's not that unusual in a lake that size, plus during a storm and that time of year. Unless you know something I don't?"

"No, it's just that..." He rubbed his neck again. "I never told anyone, but Laura was insanely jealous."

"Insanely?" the sheriff asked.

"It was what we were fighting about the day she drowned," Hoyt said, his voice full of pain. "She attacked me. I was trying to hold her off...." He let out a sound like a sob.

Emma closed her eyes and leaned into the side of the house. The wood felt cool to the touch. She wanted to run to her husband, throw her arms around him, comfort him. She knew what was coming, feared it bone deep.

"I swear to you, McCall, I didn't push her overboard," Hoyt was saying. "She pulled away from me. I thought she'd lost her balance. But the truth is...I think she might have purposely fallen overboard."

DAWSON GRABBED Jinx's hand and pulled her back into the bathroom as the bedroom door slammed open. As heavy footfalls thudded across the floor, he raised the shotgun, motioning for her to be quiet.

As if that was necessary. From Jinx's expression, he figured she was thinking the same thing he was. Lyndel had discovered that Jinx wasn't in the broom closet and now they were turning the house upside down looking for her.

Dawson listened to someone rummaging around in the bedroom. Lyndel? Slim? Or had someone else arrived? And what were they searching for in the master bedroom?

He heard a drawer close, then the familiar snick of a bullet being jacked into the chamber of a gun before the person left, slamming the door behind them. Whoever had come into the room was now armed as well as dangerous.

Dawson let out the breath he'd been holding. Getting out of there without any bloodshed was seeming less and less likely. They would be looking for Jinx inside the house and out. For all he knew, Lyndel had called in more ranch hands to help. Or possibly even the rest of the rustlers back from Montana.

He eased the bathroom door open and peered out. Jinx did the same next to him. The bedroom was empty.

The way he saw it, they had two options. Trying

to escape through the back way without the digital recorder. Or going out the front door with it.

Dawson walked over to the phone beside the bed and picked up the receiver, remembering belatedly that Lyndel had had it disconnected. He wasn't in the habit of carrying a cell phone. They were pretty worthless unless you lived in Whitehorse. A few miles out, you couldn't get any service, so what was the point when you lived on a ranch miles from town?

But he wished to hell he had one right now. He looked over at Jinx.

She shook her head. "Mine's in the other pocket of my jean jacket."

Great. "Come on," Dawson said. "We're getting out of here. We'll call the sheriff as soon as we reach town and have him get your jacket and the digital recorder with the evidence on it." He'd expected her to put up an argument and was surprised when she didn't.

For once Jinx wasn't taking chances? It gave him hope.

He moved to the door, grabbed the knob and slowly turned it. As he pulled the door open a crack, he peered out. The hallway was empty. "Stay behind me."

Jinx nodded and they slipped out of the master suite into the hallway.

Dawson could hear raised voices coming from

the front part of the house and knew any moment they would be searching the house. He hoped they'd already done a preliminary search of all of the rooms except the master suite. It was far enough off the grid that they might not have bothered with it the first time around.

He headed for the first exit they came to, stopping at the door to look back at Jinx. He figured if there was a security system installed, it would be on now.

"The moment I open this door we hightail it for that grove of trees east of the house. You lead. I'll be right behind you with the shotgun."

She nodded, looking as anxious as he was.

He shoved open the door and they sprinted across the moonlit ranch yard toward the dark grove of trees in the distance. Dawson could hear voices in the distance, the yelp of a dog. Glancing back, he saw no movement from the house.

Ahead he saw several of the horses he had released standing broadside against the dark horizon. He heard a vehicle engine rev in front of the house and more shouting.

Jinx had reached the trees. Her dark shadow blended with the deep shadows of the trees and for a moment he lost sight of her. Then something glinted in a slice of moonlight that cut down through the tree limbs and leaves.

And he saw Jinx. Lyndel had one arm locked around her throat. In the other he held a gun, the barrel catching the moonlight as he pointed it at her temple.

"Drop the shotgun, Dawson, or I'll kill her right now."

"WHAT IS THIS ABOUT Dawson getting caught in the middle of a rustling ring?" Hoyt asked his wife later as they lay in their large bed. A light breeze played at the curtains at the window. Moonlight spilled in along with summer-scented air.

Emma filled him in on what she knew, which wasn't much. "Apparently he met a woman up on the mountain. McCall thinks she was riding with the rustlers."

"Are you trying to tell me that Dawson has fallen in love with a rustler?" her husband demanded.

She hated to tell him that might be the least of it. "McCall has had to put an APB out on her for questioning. One of the rustlers' bodies was found in an old abandoned ranch house up on the mountain."

"So we don't know who killed him," Hoyt said. "Could have been one of the other rustlers. Or this woman. Or Dawson." He raked a hand through his thick blond hair. It was beginning to gray and had seemed to gray even more since Emma had come into his life, she thought with regret.

"We need to talk about the past sometime," she said. "I need to tell you about my former husband."

He took her hand and met her gaze. "I never

doubted that you had a past, Emma. If you want to tell me about it, fine. But I'm not asking. I don't need to know. I know you."

She smiled. "Yours might not be the only past that comes back to haunt us, but it can wait for now."

He nodded. "Tell me what you know about this woman rustler, then."

"Apparently she had gone undercover to bring down the rustling ring."

Hoyt raised a brow. "And almost got my son killed."

Emma couldn't argue that. "I've always known it would take a special woman for each of your 'boys,'" she said, smiling over at her husband. Like her husband, though, she feared that this woman Dawson had gone after might get them both killed before this was over. "You know your son."

He swore under his breath. "Yes," he said and started to get out of bed.

"Where do you think you're going?" she demanded.

"I have cattle to help round up, a son to find—"

She caught his hand. "Hoyt, they aren't boys anymore. They've been running this ranch just fine without you. They can run it a few more hours without your help. Anyway, it's too late to do anything tonight and you know it."

He smiled down at her, then came back to bed, taking her in his arms. She thought about what she'd overheard him telling the sheriff and pushed the thought away. No one other than Aggie was involved in what had happened.

Laura might have been *insanely* jealous, but Aggie was apparently just plain insane. At least she was locked up where she couldn't hurt anyone else, Emma thought as she snuggled into her husband's strong, warm body.

"PUT DOWN THE SHOTGUN, Dawson," Lyndel said again.

"Don't listen to him," Jinx said. "He can't kill me and get away with it."

Lyndel laughed. "That's only if her body is ever found."

Jinx saw movement at the edge of the trees. "Dawson, look out!"

But the warning didn't come quickly enough. Two men sprang from the trees behind him, wrenched the shotgun away and threw him to the ground.

"Don't hurt him," she cried. "He doesn't have anything to do with this."

"Bring him along," Lyndel ordered. "He sealed his fate when he threw in with you." He grabbed her arm roughly and shoved her back toward the house. "I knew he wouldn't just go away and leave well enough alone. Apparently he got himself *jinxed* by the likes of you and now it is going to cost him his life."

To her surprise, Lyndel didn't take them to the house but to his Cadillac running out front. He shoved her into the front seat at gunpoint and climbed in after her. Dawson was thrown into the backseat with one of Lyndel's men, also at gunpoint, as Slim slipped behind the wheel.

Out of habit, Jinx reached for her seat belt.

"You won't be needing that," Lyndel said with a chuckle.

She snapped it on anyway, making him shake his head.

"Take us to the quarry," he ordered.

Jinx swallowed as she realized what he had planned. He wasn't joking about their bodies never being found. The rock quarry on the ranch had filled in with water years ago. As a girl she'd been warned not to go there because the water was so cold and deep. She knew Lyndel hadn't heeded warnings about it and had almost drowned there one summer. The girl who'd been with him had drowned and Hank Thompson had fenced the quarry, adding several strings of barbed wire along the top and locking the gate in.

The headlights cut a swath of golden light on the narrow ranch road. There was no other ranch within miles, no one around out here in the middle of nowhere. Jinx thought of Dawson in the backseat. He'd come after her and now it was going to cost him his life. She couldn't let that happen. No matter what she had to do.

Slim slowed and turned down an even narrower dirt road. In the moonlight she could see the tall cottonwoods around the quarry. The light glinted off the steel fence Lyndel's father had built around the deep, water-filled hole.

Large rocks rose up from the edges of the quarry. Slim pulled up to the gate and got out to unlock it.

Jinx's mind raced. She had to do something desperate. This time her situation actually demanded it. Lyndel was going to kill them either way, so she didn't see that she had anything to lose. She glanced in the rearview mirror, saw Dawson. Their gazes met and she tried to send a silent message.

Slim returned, slid behind the seat and shifted the car into gear as he pulled through the open gate. Lyndel must have been selling the quarry stone again, because this end of the quarry sloped down to the water and she could see where workers had been blasting.

"Drive down to the edge," Lyndel ordered.

Moonlight shone on the dark surface of the cold, deep water as Slim drove closer to the edge and what appeared to be no more than a fifteen-foot drop to the water at this end.

As Slim started to slow, Jinx shot Dawson a glance, then slipped her foot over and tromped on the gas. She heard Dawson snap on his seat belt. Jinx had hoped she could catch Slim by surprise. But she couldn't take the chance that he would go for the brake. Or even throw the car into Reverse.

Fortunately Slim wasn't quick, not mentally or physically, and she had managed to catch him by surprise. She'd also shoved against him, slamming him into his door as she tromped on his big foot on the gas pedal, throwing him off balance enough that he didn't recover before it was too late.

Beside her, Lyndel let out a curse and grabbed for her, latching on to her arm to pull her back toward him, then quickly letting go as the car soared over the edge and began a nosedive for the water below. Jinx braced herself and prayed that she hadn't just killed them all.

DAWSON COULDN'T BELIEVE IT. When he'd looked into Jinx's eyes, he'd known she was going to do something desperate. He'd been trying to come up with something himself, since it was clear what Lyndel had planned for them when he realized what she was going to do.

He braced himself as the engine revved and he felt the vehicle go airborne. It seemed to hang in the air, then did a slow nosedive, rolling forward. The ranch hand who'd been beside him flew forward along the headliner as they struck the water with a force that shook Dawson's teeth.

The car plunged, then bobbed up as it flipped over

on its top. Everything went quiet except for the slosh of waves against the sides of the car and the sound of the water rushing in.

Dawson found himself alone, suspended upside down by his seat belt in the backseat. "Jinx?" he cried, seeing her hanging, as well. The others seemed to be piled on the windshield upfront, none of them moving. At least not yet.

He quickly unsnapped his seat belt and dropped to the interior roof of the car. Hurriedly he crawled to the front. Water was rushing into the car at every crack and crevice. His movements made the car pitch as if it was a boat. A sinking boat.

Jinx was fumbling with her seat belt.

"Are you all right?"

She nodded. He saw that there was a cut over her eye and it was bleeding. He helped her unsnap the belt and lowered her to the headliner, which was now already soaked with water.

One of the ranch hands or Lyndel moaned. They'd all been thrown into the windshield. The water around them was turning red with their blood.

Dawson looked around for something to break out one of the windows, as the water seemed to be coming in faster, leaving less air space. It wouldn't be long before the weight of the water would sink the car.

He spotted his shotgun and remembered Slim picking it up and carrying it toward the car. "I'm going to bust out the back window, but when I do the water is going to rush in. We won't be able to swim out until it fills the car."

Jinx nodded.

"Hang on to the seat. Hold your breath, then take my hand, okay?" He met her gaze. "We're going to get out of this."

Another groan from the front of the car. Hurriedly Dawson took a swing at the back window with the butt of the shotgun, his back to what was happening behind him.

DAWSON DIDN'T SEE LYNDEL push himself away from Slim and the other man, both of them unmoving. But the movement caught Jinx's eye. She watched in horror as Lyndel's hand snaked out and latched on to a gun that had been lying at the edge of the bodies.

"You really are a jinx," he said, his words slurred, his eyes wild.

"Dawson!" she cried as Lyndel lifted the gun and aimed it at her head.

Dawson was already in midswing with the butt of the shotgun. He started to turn when the glass shuddered. The water came rushing in like a tidal wave. Jinx saw Lyndel's eyes widen as Dawson was washed back toward them. Lyndel might have gotten off a shot. Jinx didn't know. If he did, the shot went wild. The wave surrounded her, slamming her back against the seat she'd been holding on to as the car quickly filled with water and began to sink.

The water was colder than anything Jinx had ever felt in her life. It stole the breath she'd been holding and she was sure she would drown. But then she felt Dawson take her hand and he was swimming her out through the gaping hole where the back window had been.

She could see moonlight above them. Her lungs felt as if they would burst. They weren't going to make it. The surface was farther than they'd thought. She felt his hand tighten on hers and a moment later they burst to the surface.

Jinx gasped for breath, choking and crying.

"You're all right," Dawson said as he pulled her to him.

She couldn't catch her breath and the cold had seeped into her bones, leaving her numb. He drew her over to the edge of the rock quarry and pulled them both up the rock ledge and into the warmth of the summer night and his strong arms.

"It's over, Brittany Bo. You're safe and I'm never letting you out of my arms ever again."

Epilogue

"I'd like to make a toast." Everyone turned their attention to Hoyt Chisholm at the head of the table. "We've had one interesting year so far and it isn't even half over." He raised his glass. "Here's hoping the next six months aren't half as eventful."

Everyone said, "Hear, hear," and raised their glasses.

Emma smiled across the table at her soon-to-be daughter-in-law, Halley. The deputy had eyes only for her fiancé, Colton, though. She was smiling up at him as they touched glasses.

Next to them Dawson and Jinx were also smiling at each other. Dawson hadn't let her out of his sight after everything that had happened to them. Emma shivered at even the thought of the two of them underwater with killers in the quarry in Wyoming. She gave a silent thanks to God that they had survived, and that the men who had been trying to kill them had perished—only because she didn't want Jinx and Dawson to have to go through a lengthy trial.

Emma liked Jinx. She was a good strong woman, capable and smart. She'd had the good sense to get Lyndel Thompson's confession on a digital recorder, which she and Dawson had given to the sheriff in Wyoming. The rustlers had been rounded up and were facing serious charges in connection with Jinx's father's murder.

Across the table, Tanner and Billie Rae were sharing a private toast of their own. Emma loved the way Billie Rae seemed to radiate with happiness when she was with Tanner. He'd said he'd fallen in love with her at first sight. Emma loved nothing better than a happy ending.

"It's been a good year so far, too," Emma added after everyone had taken a drink of their champagne. She'd thought that the night had called for prime rib from one of their beef and champagne and all the trimmings. "We have a lot of celebrate, including those who have joined us tonight."

She lifted her glass to Colton and Halley, then Jinx and Dawson, then Tanner and Billie Rae, turning to smile down the long table at Sheriff McCall Crawford and her husband, Luke. The sheriff was glowing and Emma wondered if it was possible...

She turned back to her own husband. As she touched his glass, her eyes locked with his. A silent look of love and relief passed between them.

"To even happier times," she said, followed by applause.

"Now can we please eat?" Marshall joked.

Emma loved the sound of laughter around the table as her gaze took in her other stepsons. Zane had gone clear to California looking for her. Her father had said how lucky she was to have such wonderful stepsons. Didn't she know it.

Next to him, Logan seemed lost in thought. Of the six, he puzzled her. She knew he loved the ranch, but as they said, he definitely heard a different drummer, with his long hair and his love of his motorcycle over horses. Emma knew he was also a puzzle to his father, but she had great hopes for him.

She'd seen a change in Marshall after everything that had happened and wondered what had caused it. He was now in the process of remodeling the farmhouse where he lived. It was part of the Chisholm Cattle Company, the most isolated of the places.

When she'd first married into the family only months ago, she'd been determined to bring the family together and she'd had this crazy idea of finding each of her stepsons the perfect mate.

She chuckled at her naïveté. Three of them had found mates in the least likely places. Emma had tried to help things along with Colton and even a little with Tanner, but she'd had nothing to do with getting Dawson and Jinx together.

Not that she had given up matchmaking. *No,* she thought as she looked at the three stepsons who were still single. She was making no promises. Now that her own life had settled down, the cattle all rounded up, Hoyt cleared of any criminal charges and Aggie soon to be headed for the state mental hospital, Emma thought she might see what she could do to help Cupid along for Marshall, Zane and Logan. Look how happy the other three were! she thought.

"SHE SHOULDN'T GIVE YOU any trouble," the deputy said as Aggie Wells was loaded into the back of the state mental hospital van. "Doc gave her something to calm her down."

The driver glanced back at the woman in his rear-view mirror, but made a point of not making eye contact.

"You must be new," the deputy said.

"Just started yesterday," the driver said. "Needed a job and this was all I could find."

"I guess there are worse jobs," the deputy agreed. "At least it's not the middle of winter where you have to fight icy roads and blowing and drifting snow a lot of the times. Good luck," he said as he started to close the van door.

"Thanks. I hope I don't need it." As he pulled away, he saw the deputy go back inside the sheriff's department.

He didn't look at the woman again until they were out of Whitehorse and headed across the open prairie. It was twilight, the sun somewhere behind the Little Rockies and the Bear Paw Mountains.

The driver checked his side mirror first. No cars behind him and none ahead as far as he could see. This really was an isolated part of the state—even during tourist season in the summer.

He finally glanced back at his passenger. "How are you doing, Aggie?"

She looked up, her gaze meeting his. "Okay, now that you're here."

He hadn't had a choice when he'd gotten her message. He owed her and had told her a long time ago that if she ever needed him... Years ago she'd proved that his wife had been systematically selling off the jewelry he gave her and replacing it with fakes, which she then paid her boyfriend to steal so she could collect on the insurance money.

He'd gotten rid of the boyfriend, kept the wife and gone into business with her. They had a nice life and he didn't have any more trouble with his wife after she'd seen what he'd done to her boyfriend.

Aggie Wells? Well, he was indebted to her in a big way.

"Did you have trouble getting the van?" she asked.

"Nothing I couldn't handle."

* * * * *

Harlequin

INTRIGUE

COMING NEXT MONTH

Available August 9, 2011

#1293 SOVEREIGN SHERIFF
Cowboys Royale
Cassie Miles

#1294 STAMPEDED
Whitehorse, Montana: Chisholm Cattle Company
B.J. Daniels

#1295 FLASHBACK
Gayle Wilson

#1296 PROTECTING THE PREGNANT WITNESS
The Precinct: SWAT
Julie Miller

#1297 LOCKED AND LOADED
Mystery Men
HelenKay Dimon

#1298 DAKOTA MARSHAL
Jenna Ryan

REQUEST YOUR FREE BOOKS!
2 FREE NOVELS PLUS 2 FREE GIFTS!

◆ Harlequin®

INTRIGUE®

BREATHTAKING ROMANTIC SUSPENSE

Once bitten, twice shy. That's Gabby Wade's motto—
especially when it comes to Adamson men.
And the moment she meets Jon Adamson her theory
is confirmed. But with each encounter a little something
sparks between them, making her wonder if she's been
too hasty to dismiss this one!

Enjoy this sneak peek from ONE GOOD REASON
by Sarah Mayberry, available August 2011
from Harlequin® Superromance®.

Gabby Wade's heartbeat thumped in her ears as she marched to her office. She wanted to pretend it was because of her brisk pace returning from the file room, but she wasn't that good a liar.

Her heart was beating like a tom-tom because Jon Adamson had touched her. In a very male, very possessive way. She could still feel the heat of his big hand burning through the seat of her khakis as he'd steadied her on the ladder.

It had taken every ounce of self-control to tell him to unhand her. What she'd really wanted was to grab him by his shirt and, well, explore all those urges his touch had instantly brought to life.

While she might not like him, she was wise enough to understand that it wasn't always about liking the other person. Sometimes it was about pure animal attraction.

Refusing to think about it, she turned to work. When she'd typed in the wrong figures three times, Gabby admitted she was too tired and too distracted. Time to call it a day.

As she was leaving, she spied Jon at his workbench in the shop. His head was propped on his hand as he studied blueprints. It wasn't until she got closer that she saw his eyes were shut.

He looked oddly boyish. There was something innocent and unguarded in his expression. She felt a weakening in her resistance to him.

"Jon." She put her hand on his shoulder, intending to shake him awake. Instead, it rested there like a caress.

His eyes snapped open.

"You were asleep."

"No, I was, uh, visualizing something on this design." He gestured to the blueprint in front of him then rubbed his eyes.

That gesture dealt a bigger blow to her resistance. She realized it wasn't only animal attraction pulling them together. She took a step backward as if to get away from the knowledge.

She cleared her throat. "I'm heading off now."

He gave her a smile, and she could see his exhaustion.

"Yeah, I should, too." He stood and stretched. The hem of his T-shirt rose as he arched his back and she caught a flash of hard male belly. She looked away, but it was too late. Her mind had committed the image to permanent memory.

And suddenly she knew, for good or bad, she'd never look at Jon the same way again.

Find out what happens next in ONE GOOD REASON, available August 2011 from Harlequin® Superromance®!

Celebrating

$\mathcal{B}laze$ **10** *years of*

red-hot reads

Featuring a special August author lineup of
six fan-favorite authors who have written
for Blaze™ from the beginning!

The Original Sexy Six:

Vicki Lewis Thompson
Tori Carrington
Kimberly Raye
Debbi Rawlins
Julie Leto
Jo Leigh

Pick up all six Blaze™
Special Collectors' Edition titles!

August 2011

MYSTERY UNRAVELED
Find the answers to the puzzles in last month's INTRIGUE titles!

Hidden Word
(Writing & Computers)

¹ T	A	B
² C	A	P
³ N	I	B

⁴ L	⁵ D	⁶ A
A	E	L
B	L	T

Hidden Word: TABLET

Hidden Word
(House)

¹ P	O	T
² P	A	N
³ C	A	N

⁴ T	⁵ F	⁶ B
I	R	A
N	Y	Y

Hidden Word: PANTRY

Figure Counting
(Squares & Rectangles)

Thirty-eight

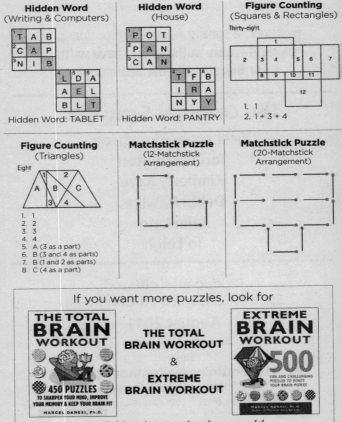

1. 1
2. 1 + 3 + 4

Figure Counting
(Triangles)

Eight

1. 1
2. 2
3. 3
4. 4
5. A (3 as a part)
6. B (3 and 4 as parts)
7. B (1 and 2 as parts)
8. C (4 as a part)

Matchstick Puzzle
(12-Matchstick Arrangement)

Matchstick Puzzle
(20-Matchstick Arrangement)

HNFPZAN2011MM